Murder in the Language Lab

Asesinato en el laboratorio de idiomas

Alm@ Pérez

Dual Language Edition

Translation by
John W. Warren

Murder in the Language Lab
Asesinato en el laboratorio de idiomas

Spanish-language version (revised):
Copyright 2016 by Tina Escaja

Translation:
Copyright © 2016 by John W. Warren

ISBN: 978-0-9979423-2-3   (Print)
ISBN: 978-0-9979423-3-0   (eBook)

Book design by John W. Warren

Cover image is a derivative of "Language Lab" by Tom in NYC
(https://flic.kr/p/dthYL), used and modified under CC-by-2.0

Published by BrookTree Media
Takoma Park, MD

Printed in the United States of America

Contents

Murder in the Language Lab

The body had appeared, throat slashed, between booths twelve and thirteen in the language laboratory, with an obscene design carved into the right buttock. The crude tattoo showed an erect penis pierced by a syringe. Wild theories of feminist vengeance floated about: a group of anti-establishment extremists brandishing syringes against the homophobic behinds of the Spanish faculty. While reporters snapped photographs and crude jokes, I discreetly approached the lab's supervisor, a small, half-balding man who eyed me suspiciously as I asked him questions about the dead man.

He didn't know the victim that well, but said he'd seen him on numerous occasions rummaging through the tapes on Italian and the audiovisual materials. He'd sometimes spent hours in the little booths staring at subtitled movies. From his choices, he didn't seem to have any particular favorites. On the night of the murder, he'd chosen a film from China, subsidized by the country's Ministry of Culture, which gave a sly defense of the communist government. That was the type of movie, along with those by Almodóvar, which seemed to dominate the list of films that the deceased, professor Martínez, had devoured during the last couple of months.

Augusto Javier Martínez, professor of nineteenth century Spanish literature at Midwest College, was originally from a small town near Guadalajara, Spain. Oppressed by his abusive parents and provincial upbringing, Martínez had decided to apply for a scholarship offered through a bank to an exchange program at a university in the southern United States. The prospect had always fascinated him. America, with the glory of John Wayne movies and the exalted perfume of Marilyn. Ah, Marilyn, myth of the fifties dominating his imagination and the white wall of his ordered apartment.

The cook, Mrs. Maria Smith, wasn't too familiar with the professor's routine, but he always seemed suspicious to her, thanks to her innate sense of distrust. "*Pobresito* Professor Martínez, always at home, always in front of *la computadora. Señor* very *esmart* and *reservao*, always something *un poquito* strange." That morning when he'd checked his mail, he'd seemed odd, even more than usual.

Rummaging through his wastebasket, I recovered a note the local police had clumsily overlooked. Miroir Pub, 142 Pine. That's where I went, at eight in the evening, hoping to clear up some of the mess into which my friend Pedro had gotten me involved.

I'd gotten out of private detective work some time ago, for reasons irrelevant here. Recently I had decided to reenter academic life, a way of life that I'd abandoned sick to death of the suffocating politics of the many departments with which I'd been involved. Professor Martínez' death interested me because we'd shared many of the same frustrations. I'd also been born in a tiny town in the Spanish countryside, and grew up on the outskirts of Madrid in a working class neighborhood where my parents had installed themselves for life. There in Madrid is where I had been a private investigator, more for amusement than for the meager and inconsistent earnings it provided. I was fascinated by the sordidness of passionate encounters and separations. I loved the sense of peril between the stench of vomit in sleazy neighborhoods and the perfume of ladies who appeared in fashion magazines. All that ended though, when I came to the USA, escaping my ghosts like everyone else who comes to this strange paradise.

So, in reality, my good friend Pedro didn't have to insist that I take the case. His company, a publisher of religious and sensationalistic tracts that also employed professor Martínez from time to time, had offered me a not insignificant sum as an advance to the rights for the morbid market that they served. They were keenly interested in having someone from the academic world to shine a light into an obscure case that the local police would kick around for awhile before calling it closed as long as no other incident occurred. For its part, the University, a tiny provincial college, would do what it could to bury such an unpleasant incident, to be ignored as soon as the next scandal came along. Since by happenstance I was already prowling around the region near Midwest College, it took only a couple of hours before I was face-to-face to the crime.

The Miroir was a small bar just off the main street and only artery of that so-called town. I sat down next to the window in order to watch the oversized cars and dilapidated trucks cruising the street slowly from one end of town to the other. From my vantage point, I could see its limits. Beyond this stretch of road there was absolutely nothing. The violet horizon divided by telegraphic staffs repeated itself into infinity. How a crime could be committed in such a sterile context was something that seemed very strange, or perfectly logical, depending on how you look at it.

Around 8:30, a burly man sporting a Yankees cap walked in and sat down at the bar. The bartender, a tall woman with oriental features and a strong accent, automatically slid over a glass of beer that the grimy man tossed down in a gulp. His pants barely covered his ample buttocks, causing him to sporadically give them a tug with a mechanical gesture. He looked over at my table and smiled while simultaneously letting out a belch. I smiled back, feigning a barroom flirt, or a cheap whore. The lump walked up, spitting out "Can I sit down, doll?" With a heavy motion he sat down, blocking a section of the street.

I pretended I was an immigrant from south of the border, while he, George Puckey, told me his non-story. Finally, I was able to steer the coarse conversation around to his daily patronage of the Miroir. He told the place was a rave, and gave me a wink. With a thick index finger stained with motor oil, he pointed out a door that would otherwise have passed totally unnoticed. I agreed to follow him to the door, my senses alert, just in case. Inside, in the semi-darkness, a bar that was the faithful twin of the one we had left behind waited in the shadows and silence like an animal in repose. While I pretended not to fathom the purpose of this other bar, the hulk began to fondle my rear. He hinted that on certain nights there were illegal deals: whores, drugs, queers, marijuana, oh baby you're so nice. Jerk. Before leaving, feigning indignation, I give him my telephone number, since despite his impertinence I kind of liked the guy, and it wouldn't be too bad to smoke a joint together in the other side of the bar on Pine Street. Half annoyed and half satisfied, the monster gave me an imperfect, yellow smile without taking his eyes off my tits. Fine, baby, I like a challenge.

I had two hours until closing time at the audiovisual lab that had finally been freed from the public's curiosity, and had no trace left of a corpse. I began to take in the films from the dead prof's pile. Earphones, VCR, and a young woman appearing and disappearing in the political-romantic plights of pre-revolutionary China. A girl with libertarian longings in a society that oppresses her as a woman and as an individual. And those close-ups, Hollywood style, of her full mouth and soft body, devoid of the stereotypical fragility of the oriental woman.

And Almodóvar, striking, parodying, pulling the leg of every presumptuous Spaniard. Sweetening it with garish colors: now a wig, now a game of gender exchange in which nothing is as it seems. And Bibi Andersen's body reflectling changes in the light.

I lug the remaining tapes to the apartment that Pedro had found for me. Hypnotized by the unfurling shapes and colors, I watch until past five in the morning. Four hours later, I'm breakfasting with the Chairwoman of the Romance Languages department.

Croissant, scrambled eggs, and tomato juice with pepper and salt. Alicia Jiménez, originally from Murcia, a professor of Peninsular literature and a specialist on contemporary female poets, seems prone to confessions.

"It's not easy for a woman to be a leader in this man's world, as you must know very well. And to this we have to add the traditional tension between the French and Spanish sections." (I take a bite out of my croissant.) "Our department has been systematically dominated by the French, contrary to the social reality in this country where Spanish is clearly more significant. It's like the system is conspiring to deny the tremendous potential and history of our culture... Ultimately... they gave me the position of Chair perhaps only because I am a Spanish woman, can you believe it?" She pauses dramatically. "Only because I represent, in this game of stereotypes, the symbols of imperialism and so on. A real piece of shit."

"But perhaps now you have the power to change those stereotypes, no?" I say in a friendly tone, encouraged by her initiative, which I'm used to no doubt since my short and chubby stature invites informality and even pats on the ass.

Dr. Alicia Jiménez is tall, wears heavy makeup, and has little blue bags under her eyes that bring to mind nights of insomnia. She dresses in a style that around here can be called "European," that is, not easily identifiable with the normal appearance of women in the American Midwest, with their sculptured, permed hair, western style during the week, flowers and lace around the neck on Sundays. Dr. Jiménez, on the contrary, wears pleated slacks and a gray blouse that faintly allows her white bra to be seen through the fabric. After a discussion of postmodern poets, she finally mentions Martínez.

"An odd duck, really. He kept to himself inside and out of the department. He hardly ever participated in the social activities we organize. For example, every first Friday of the month we have a... social gathering, that is, a little party in which we have wine and cheese and to which we invite the very few graduate students that we have. Now that I remember, of the two or three times that Martínez came to the chats, one was last Friday."

"Who else came to the party?"

"The usual ones. Mario, specialist in Colonial lit. Skilling, Medievalist. His wife, Susana, also Medievalist. Philippe, James and Mary from French.... I'll give you a list if you'd like."

"Which of the grad students came?"

"Miguel, I mean Michael Keith, one of the regulars. Dynamic, though a bit scatterbrained. He's been here longer than the bishop, I mean longer than Dr. Johnson. Let's see, I don't really know the names of the French students... But also last Friday, Miguel's girlfriend came, Chan Li. Unusual, since that girl's so timid she can barely handle the hypocrisy in our pedantic conversations. In reality, the parties are mainly for ourselves, and for our delicate egos, and we unconsciously exclude any of the graduate students whose enthusiasm reminds us of our own fruitless ideals. As for us, professors in the middle of nowhere, we know that despite our pretensions we're only a bunch of B-movie dinosaurs."

Before utterly losing her to melancholic contemplation, I wanted to bring her back down to the table in the University cafeteria where my second cup of weak coffee had become cold.

"This Chan Li... Was she a student of Spanish or French?"

"Spanish. And, incidentally, she was doing her dissertation under Martínez. I don't know what she's going to do now, poor thing. This late, and with the MLA conference approaching."

"Where does she live?"

"In the women's dormitory. Around here, they're so puritanical that they have separate dormitories for boys and girls. At 11:00 each night everyone of the opposite sex has to leave the respective dormitory. Ridiculous. The funny thing is that, actually, the number of student pregnancies has been considerably reduced since this rule was applied. Paternalistic worries can't ignore the sexual promiscuity of these children, after all, who despite their false liberty are still overprotected. They're barely allowed to grow up..."

Before leaving, I drank the rest of my coffee with disgust and added a couple of dollars to the generous tip. "Don't worry about it," she insisted with a gesture of complicity, adding, "the department takes care of the tip as well."

Chan Li shared a room with a corpulent Caucasian woman who moved with an agility that belied her weight. Li occupied the lower part of the room, which appeared unadorned and in meticulous order, filled only with essentials, delicate and conventional items. An upstairs loft concealed the other woman's disorder. The room smelled of canned stew that the latter had doubtlessly prepared on a hotplate, ignoring the dormitory's prohibition on cooking in bedrooms. After apologizing for a tremendous belch that reminded me of George, the roommate, Shannon, told me that Chan Li was most likely with Michael in the library's computer section, as tomorrow was the application deadline for an important grant that Li was hoping to receive. So that's where I headed.

Spring seemed like just the ticket for the guys and gals flashing public-relations smiles in collective pride. Their movements were mellow or hasty, depending on the students' tight schedules. Dodging bicycles and neutral greetings, I arrived at the mass of the library, distinguishable from its boring, rectangular style and from the wide staircases on which some young people bathed in the sun. After struggling with the staff at the entrance, who literally x-rayed my tawny self in those halls of knowledge, I finally found the computer room situated on the fifth floor.

They were easy to spot in that large room filled with baseball caps whose owners toiled with fingers banging away on computer keyboards. A few hours more and the torture of homework would be finished, and almost everyone, caps in reverse, would enjoy a well-deserved Friday afternoon beer. Almost none, of course, had reached the requisite twenty-one years for alcohol consumption.

Chan Li fixed her gaze on me as I approached. Her face was rounded and her eyes were swollen. Her complexion was dark and her lips thick and sensual. Mike/Miguel caressed her back in a vertical motion, eyes fixed solidly on the blue screen of the terminal, completely lost in thought. It was the final section of the difficult application. Among the official forms scattered about on the next table, I could make out the signature of the dissertation director, Dr. Martínez.

I introduced myself as a candidate for graduate school in Spanish, and asked them to give me their honest opinion about the department. Miguel's voice immediately took a confessional tone as he answered.

"Well, you'll find this is a small department, there are few interesting specialists. What field are you interested in?"

"I'm not sure yet. I'm interested in the modern period, especially turn-of-the-century culture," I ventured.

I knew that Martínez' work was on the 19th century, but I hadn't yet checked into his latest research.

"What a coincidence! That's exactly what Li is applying for, a grant for research on the turn-of-the-century."

"I'd love to know about that project."

Li appeared suspicious for a moment, but finally relented. "My work connects the end of the 19th century with the end of the 20th. The crisis, epidemic metaphors of sexual origin, like syphilis and AIDS, respectively..."

"HIV," corrected Mike/Miguel. Li didn't seem to appreciate the interruption.

"HIV," Chan Li corrected herself, "I think it's a topic with a lot of potential."

"That's what your dissertation is on?" I ventured.

"Yes," she answered, and it seemed as if her gaze darkened slightly.

"And how is your dissertation going?" I insisted.

She seemed a little unhappy about the question and Mike decided to answer. "Now she's stuck, she needs to change her dissertation director but, as we said, there aren't many specialists in the department. Her ex-director was a monster in the field. He was kind of a creep but he had a lot of talent, overall. *Joder!* The shithead fell head over heals for Li. He totally had the hots for her, even though I always thought he seemed kind of gay. *Coño!*"

Mike prided himself on his assured Spanish admirably learned on a lengthy scholarly visit to Spain. To emphasize his supremacy he often adorned his verbiage with swear words that didn't quite belong. Li seemed a little disoriented. Finally, she decided to speak once more, studiously avoiding the matter her friend had just broached.

"I might change topics. I know at this point that's probably not too smart, but I don't feel comfortable now after... I have to make a presentation at MLA in December and I have to decide. Right now, I think it's worth trying to get some security with this application to the government."

"Seems like a good idea," I agreed.

I arrived home totally wiped out. The answering machine's blinking light indicated three messages. The first was from Pedro. How am I doing, that he'd call later. The second was from George, inviting me, I believe, on a date that same night. I had to rewind the message three times to understand a thing. The third message was just a long silence. Evidently, the caller didn't want to hang up nor talk, trying to somehow make me nervous. Just as I was about to lie in bed for a moment, the phone rings. I hesitate a moment before deciding to answer. Through the phone line, Pedro's unmistakable greeting.

"Hey *chica*, *cómo estás*? God, you're impossible to get a hold of. How's it going?"

"So, so, but I need some information from you."

"Whatever you need. But first, I've got some bad news for you. The company that asked me to hire you has lost interest in the Martínez case. They're interested, it seems, in some other case that happened on the East Coast that's perfect for their sensationalistic section. Some woman who castrated her husband... Spicy. But tell me."

"As long as they pay me... Listen, you've got to tell me what the deceased was interested in recently and what he was doing for your publishing company."

"Martínez had recently become interested in the socio-sexual theory, or something like that, at the turn of the last century. Crisis, venereal diseases, decadence, etc. He wrote an occasional pseudo-philosophical column in the magazine where he combined observations on crimes of passion with theory on cinema. I'll send them to you if you'd like."

"Kind of a weird guy."

"He was a great guy. A bit nuts. He had these ideas about he'd change the world and ignite the younger generation... Oh, he also wrote poems."

"Poems?"

"Yeah, and they were as strange and dark as his prose."

"How was his love life?"

"Very discreet. No one ever knew a thing about a relationship of any sort, and there was a bit of speculation about his sexual orientation."

"I see... How's your sabbatical going?"

"Awesome, but, as you can see, I'm missing the juicy bits."

"You're the lucky one, I'd say. But look, this call's going to cost you a fortune from Florida."

"The company will cover it. Business, you know..."

"Yeah, yeah. I know. Well anyway, talk to you soon. Take it easy."

"All right, we'll talk soon, and hurry up with the case because these guys are fickle. Good luck, *guapa*."

"Chao."

Nine p.m. on a Friday night. I searched my suitcase for the tackiest thing I could find. I loaded up on the makeup. Unconsciously, I concentrated on the line above the eyes, giving them a bit of an almond shape. Crimson on the lips and lots of rouge. Red and black, perfect.

It was still a half hour before my date with George but I wanted to check out the area beforehand by myself. I sat at the same table in the Miroir, from where I was able to watch the covert activity beyond the hidden door. The bartender, who looked oriental, looked at me occasionally. She seemed slightly disgusted. She disappeared and was replaced by a man with a generous mustache who moved with languid gestures. The bar seemed slightly different, like a strange reflection in a mirror. Opposite the bar on the other side, beyond the hidden door, the room in which I now waited: young guys with hats guzzling beer, gals in jeans with tight shirts and white sneakers. In truth, my get up made me look totally out of place. In front of my tall glass of beer, I waited.

George arrived twenty minutes late. He came up to the table and tried to give me a smooch that I deflected toward my glass of beer. He thought the gesture was funny and laughed loudly. He grabbed me by the arm and led me toward the hidden door.

"Not her!" ordered the barmaid, who was now standing guard near the door. She definitely didn't like me.

"She's going in 'cause I damn well feel like it," George the brute said, I think, launching a muffled bellow saturated in alcohol toward the woman's face. Unperturbed, the guardian tucked back a stray lock of hair, moved to one side, and, glaring at me, let us through.

Beyond the door, what looked like a strip-tease show was just beginning. A young woman appeared in the darkness of the stage illuminated by a faint ray of light. She was dressed in ripped black leather laced together by thongs and clasps that tried to give an aggressive appearance to her diminutive, almost pubescent, body. She began her dance with vaguely obscene and sinuous motions that cut into the faint beam of light. From where I stood, I could only see her eyes, and study her face highlighted by heavy red lipstick. She untied one of the straps, leaving bare one of her white, impeccable arms. She repeated the cadence with the other arm and with her legs. The public began to get excited and began to bellow like George, or maybe it was George's own bellowing repeated in the mirrored echo of darkness.

When she began to caress her small breasts, the muse's delicate hand reached up to the top strap of the bodice. She paused before each new beat of unlacing, gradually disrobing. When she seemed finished with her torso, her hands remained over what remained of the leather bodice, hiding her breasts. Meanwhile, she moistened her lips with a flexible and perfectly complicit tongue-mollusk.

With her back toward the darkness of the audience, she rips off the bodice, holding it aloft in her right hand, extended like her taut, open legs. Her ass revolves in a wide circle that she keeps facing the crowd, which has become something in between spellbound and bestial by the decidedly seductive spectacle. Fascinated as I am, I try to concentrate on discerning her face.

Just when it looked as if the strip tease was coming to an end, another figure emerges, indeterminate, unclassifiable. The girl continues with her back toward the public in her axial position. The other closes in and begins to caress her, first with one hand, visibly, working like the imagination of the excited audience. Moving behind the girl, the partner begins to trace her body with a tongue, commencing at the nape after separating her straight, black hair, and following the line of her back down to her ass and to her sex sheathed in glistening, black leather. Kneeling, lingering, tongue over the nether regions of the girl, who evidently enjoys it, her rhythmic dance now accompanied by soft moans of pleasure.

They can't take any more! The Americans are climbing the walls of their supercharged minds and George gropes my ass without the slightest inhibition.

The licker also has long, straight hair, but is taller, much taller than the girl. Finally, the taller one softly, delicately removes the last bit of clothing from the pubescent figure by untying the leather crotch-piece. Free of this, the girl shows off her small, white ass and gives herself to the other, who, turning to the side for dramatic effect, suddenly begins to sodomize her in perfect timing to the music, the same music that began as a prelude to this hypnotic, sexual scene. They maintain a rhythm that gradually intensifies, and intensifies, until the expected climax, marvelously simultaneous, that coincides, of course, with the music's crescendo.

The pair look spent, and as the girl turns toward the audience I recognize the swollen eyes of the graduate student. The music and lights are switched off, extinguishing everything like the unreal spectacle of a dream.

Puzzled by the evidence, I break away from my mastodon and aim myself toward what I judge are the dressing rooms. In front of one of the doors, I again come face-to-face with the guardian, a ubiquitous presence it seems, who advances in a threatening manner.

"Get lost, or I'll cut you," she said as she fingered the spring of a switchblade, which to my eyes looked enormous. I decide to split with the taste of recognition in my mouth. Not only the strip-teasing student but also the act's other presence seems familiar. Nevertheless, I stay lurking in a corner nearby, watching. The guardian rolls a joint and begins to inhale the smoke with delight. I wouldn't mind some myself. A moment passes before she turns to open the door, and I glimpse through the opening the mournful sight of the stripper shooting-up, seemingly happy and consoled, desperately consoled, in an ineffable gesture intuited through the heavy makeup.

I notice the red "Exit" sign and escape into the night of a campus before dawn auguring another paroxysmal weekend. Sex and alcohol falsely restrained, the ecstasy of beer and rap beats that inevitably reminded me of the bar on the other side of the Miroir Bar. Groups of boys and girls wander the streets, hanging out in porticos of Doric columns from which muscular frat boys call out to party. The blue campus police patrols watch in silence.

I climb the red brick path that leads to my apartment, hoping to fight off the loneliness and alienation with which I'm saddled by those happy multitudes, and try to put some order to my thoughts. Next to my building's entrance, a grey mound asks me for coins. I rummage through my pickets and toss him some loose change. He gives me his blessing.

In the living room, the answering machine blinks again. I press the message button, which delivers a threatening, guttural voice, inviting me to a meeting on the following night. I should go alone. I go to bed with Li shooting-up and her terrible addiction replaying in my mind. The pieces were beginning to fit together somehow, but I wasn't exactly sure how. And the voice on the answering machine?

In the morning, I tried in vain to find Li. I called Miguel. We agreed to meet right away at his dormitory. It was a brilliant morning, and the campus, with few students out and about, had recovered a certain local flavor. Families came and went with ice cream cones and baby carriages, while children romped on the grass. Only echoes of the night remained in the tidy street corners. The fraternities, beasts in repose, kept a disturbing quiet.

The dormitory building in which Miguel lived consisted of a triangular complex accessed by a narrow entrance with a revolving gate. I had to identify myself with the visitor badge they'd given me for the purpose and, after a call from the duty guard, acrobatic Miguel came down to meet me. We cruised down a green esplanade where a consummate optimist played Frisbee with his dog. The frisky frolics of the animal seemed like the only vibrant tone in that serene milieu that resisted awakening. Now in his room, I mention a bit about last night's flick, and, without answering directly, he pretends not to know anything about the matter. He knew about Li's heroin addiction but said he didn't know about any other illegal activity. He obviously adored his girlfriend. He began talking about the interest Martínez had shown in his girlfriend, his comments showing a contempt and mocking that barely concealed his jealousy. He also told me that professor Martínez had written a poem to the girl and he had it somewhere in his room. The jerk.

"Why is it that you have the poem?"

He seemed taken aback.

"Well, I got it from Li. She could care less. She was totally indifferent to his flirting, but she had a lot of respect for the old guy. Let me see if I can find that little poem," and he disappeared into the adjacent room, presumably his office.

While I waited for Miguel, I amused my eyes on the mess of books, dirty clothes, file folders, notes and other objects scattered about the room. There was also a valise with makeup jars and lipstick that I supposed belonged to Chan Li, and a diverse collection of videotapes that included *Terminator*, *Star Trek*, *La Muerte de Mikel*, and *Labyrinth of Passion*. In nearly every photo hanging on the walls the girl's smile appeared: Chan Li at a sit-in protesting an increase in the University's fees, Chan Li on the women's baseball team, Chan Li with Martínez and Miguel on the beach, Chan Li with Miguel in a digital print, of poor quality, at a massive demonstration with banners in Chinese. I'm intrigued by the digital print. Miguel didn't quite fit in the scene. Under the picture's frame, forced against it nearly, I could just make out a date on the bottom right: 04 Jun 89. I'd turned back to the photo of Chan Li on the baseball team when I hear Miguel's voice behind my back.

"Oh, isn't that one great," Miguel said emphatically returning from his office. "She doesn't look like it, but Chan Li is really strong, she was usually the cleanup batter on her school's team and she was unbeatable. Unbeatable bat, funny, isn't it?"

Miguel seemed pleased with his play on words, and while roaring with laughter that seemed a bit misplaced, he told me with a forced indifference that he couldn't find the poem. "Chan Li must have it after all," he concluded.

"How long have you known Chan Li?"

"Well, since the '89–'90 term. She hardly knew English when she arrived but I helped her out with everything. She's very intelligent. She gets along well. We're going to get married soon, for the green card and all that. And we're going to get out of this shit hole."

"I thought you liked it here? You've been here for many years, haven't you?"

"Well… yeah, a few I guess. But I don't want to stay here any longer." I think he started to get a bit nervous. I decided to stick with the subject.

"And what will happen if Chan Li gets a job a long ways from here? I understand you're still having some trouble with your dissertation?"

It was pretty obvious that he didn't appreciate the comment.

"Listen, that's none of your business," he was suddenly irritated and nearly violent. "Besides, I'm pretty tired of your questions."

"Fine, fine, cool it, I'm leaving," I said, adopting a conciliatory posture. For the moment, I didn't want to reveal my real reason for my visit to Midwest College. "I'm just curious by nature," I concluded. "If you see Chan Li, tell her I'd like to talk to her."

Miguel said nothing.

I promised to return at a better time and after a quick goodbye, I headed to the office of International Studies that I supposed was closed on the weekend. So I called the person in charge, a Mr. Smith, and while he drove from his home to the campus, I took advantage of the break by lunching on an enormous salami sub chock-full of all kinds of extras and sauces. The surfeit was due to a misunderstanding, or better yet, disconnect, between the deli clerk and my limited English. I nearly always try to make things easier by saying yes to everything, and whatever happens, happens. This time what happened was colossal: mayonnaise, ketchup, mustard, onion, pickles, sweet peppers, tomato, lettuce, and some kind of red substance that I couldn't identify. All this in addition to the salami, of course. Hoping to frighten away the likely ghost of indigestion, I ate the entire sub and arrived stuffed to the gills at the office door almost simultaneously with the tall and refined Mr. Smith. The contrast between the two of us was extreme and that made me feel slightly insecure. The pickles began to give me dyspepsia. I tried to compose myself as well as I could.

"A pleasure."

"Likewise. Please, come in… Have a seat," he offered with a chilly formality. "They have asked me to help you with any information that you desire. You'll have to tell me, of course, how I might possibly be of help."

"I would like to see Chan Li's file."

He seemed surprised.

"I was under the impression that you were investigating Martinez' unfortunate… 'incident.' I don't see what that could possibly have to do with Li."

"I see that you're pretty familiar with her."

"We know all of our foreign students quite well. Chan Li is, on the other hand, a special case," he conceded, which he immediately seemed to regret. He waited for my reaction.

"And why?"

"Personal information is always confidential."

It was obvious that despite his original proclamation, Mr. Smith was resisting cooperation.

"Let me remind you that I'm investigating a murder and if you don't want to help I will be obliged to include that in my report." The parsimony and reticence of my interlocutor was beginning to piss me off.

Somewhat annoyed, the man got up from his chair and headed over to an enormous metal file cabinet behind my back. Pretending to powder my nose, an unlikely detail for anyone who knows me, but a handy one at the moment, I watched reflected in the compact's mirror the svelte gentleman's figure as he dived through the papers. He appeared to find a yellow file folder out of which he took out a few papers. He slammed the drawer closed while I in turn stashed away my little mirror. From behind my shoulder, he began to hand me the papers one by one. An aroma emanated from his dark suit that I inevitably associated with those trendy colognes that adolescents tend to use.

"Here is the application for the scholarship to study Spanish. The acceptance for entrance to the United States. Photocopies of her documents. Everything in order."

"It's my understanding that students that come from countries like China need some sort of authorization or contract from the government… I don't see any form like that here."

"…It's obvious that if we have all her immigration details in order, we would also have the papers that you are referring to… At any rate, it has nothing to do with the matter at hand," Mr. Smith continued in his condescending and evasive manner.

"I see that Chan Li is also applying for a green card. How is that possible? Foreign students without work don't have any possibility of getting residency in this country."

"I told you that Chan Li is a special case…"

"Yes, I recall, but you never told me exactly why that's the case."

Mr. Smith considered for a few seconds and began to articulate his sentences with calculated calm.

"Chan Li is a political dissident, and the University has promised to help her, but in a confidential manner. I'm sure you'll understand."

"Well, no, the truth is I don't understand. Perhaps you could be more explicit."

"You'll have to excuse me but I cannot reveal that information…" He stood up suddenly, put the papers back into the yellow folder and placed them back into the file cabinet, closing it with a key. "And now, if you'll permit me, I must return home immediately. My family is waiting for me for dinner."

"Of course."

Convinced that I'd be able to extract very little else from the reticent man, I decided to quickly get out of my chair and open the door. While ceremoniously letting Mr. Smith pass by, I discreetly turned the lock on the doorknob to leave it open. I'd decided to return to the office that very night in order to dive into Chan Li's file on my own. Mr. Smith seemed unnerved by my gesture of letting him pass first through the door, but let it go. His hesitation amused me. We said goodbye at the building's entrance with a neutral handshake.

It's getting dark. On the way to my apartment, I sense that I'm being followed. I turn around at an opportune moment, but no, I don't see anyone. Maybe it's my imagination. At the edge of campus, unprotected by passersby and patrols, I feel at my back the sound, quite close, of footsteps. I measure the cadence and confirm that they coincide with mine. They're definitely following me. But it doesn't look like anyone is behind me. I can't avoid feeling a bit nervous. I keep in my sights the blue light of the emergency phone that the University installs on the outskirts of the campus to protect its offspring; it's probably the last one in this zone. The footsteps ring out relentlessly in the deserted street and I walk faster and faster. I arrive at the phone but I decide not to stop. Only a few yards and then home. Come on, Alma, only a few yards more. I'm throbbing with the sensation of danger. I hurry on. A neighbor is about to enter the doorway of my building.

"Wait!" I shout and catch it running, visibly relieved.

As I enter, the usual shape asks me for loose change. A blurry figure disappears in the darkness.

China 1989

I'm filled with a sensation of anticipation and certainty as I press the "Enter" key on the computer. The allusive headlines appear immediately: China, 1989, Tiananmen Square crammed with hopeful students. They sit singing songs of freedom, of peace, propelled by collective energy. The multitudinous sit-in is the culmination of months of hope and struggle. From all corners of the country febrile students have arrived, convinced of the need for change, and of the power of their peaceful protest.

Suddenly tanks appear. They keep filling the streets, advancing, crushing, destroying. The soldiers begin spreading terror. The boys and girls shout, unable to avoid the brutal nightmare. Blood stays stubbornly in the street for many days. The Tiananmen massacre is history and tragedy, its images repeated inexorably on the Internet.

Still dazed, I turn off the computer and return to the darkness of my room. It's now night. The streets begin to wake from their nap. I put on tennis shoes and jeans, fasten the revolver in my waistband and cram some handcuffs into my back pocket, just in case, and slip into the groups of hung-over young people determined to repeat their Saturday night. I head quickly to the office of International Studies. This time no one appears to be following me. I enter the building with determination and, after making sure that no one is around, open the office effortlessly. I jigger the lock on the file cabinet and open it without trouble.

Lepeltier, Lewinter... Li. In Chan Li's folder are the documents that Smith showed me, as well as those that he had alluded to: political documents that accuse her of antirevolutionary collaboration. Li associated with one of the leaders of Tiananmen Square, killed in the incident. Leafing through the papers a photograph falls to the floor. I turn it over and recognize from Chan Li's expression that it's the same shot as the one that Miguel had in his room, with Tiananmen Square in the background, but here she's next to professor Martínez. Miguel had obviously scanned the photograph and substituted his own image for the professor's. I thought that Martínez, also a foreigner, must have his documents around here as well. I decided to look in the cabinet for Martínez' folder.

Augusto Javier Martínez had an enviable history. His documents, although strictly related to immigration matters, still alluded to numerous academic and humanitarian honors. During the year '87–'88, he'd been a visiting professor at the University of Hunan, in Changsha, China. Among the forms and papers regarding his visit, I found a document about Chan Li that I thought must have been misfiled, perhaps on purpose. The transcript contradicted the evidence of the photo that I'd found in Li's file, and in a way justified Mr. Smith's squeamishness…

In addition to the documents about his trip to China, in Martínez' file there were also those concerning his application for the so-called "green card," allowing the applicant legal status to work, and admitting him as a permanent resident of the United States. In the I-485 form of the application I noted an interesting dissonance to the routine negative answers, such as "In the past ten years have you been involved in prostitution, led someone into prostitution, or plan to in the future?" or "Have you been involved in espionage or are you intending to be involved in acts of espionage and/or terrorism?" The dissonance to these negatives came from the next question: "Have you ever been arrested, cited by a judge, accused, or incarcerated for breaking the law?" The answer was checked in the "Yes" box.

As I'm about to find out the motive behind Martínez' accusation and possible arrest, the door opens with a racket and two uniformed hulks pounce on me and drag me toward the exit. Along with my initial surprise, I'm struck by the ironic coincidence framed by the episode of the late professor that I was close to unraveling. Handcuffed, they throw me headfirst into the patrol car and the biggest cop gropes me in the ass. I call him an asshole.

The enclosure where they take me seems to be a kind of antechamber to the jail. My cell was small, with only a toilet, sink, and cot that seem to all be made from the same piece of metal. The surface gleamed and smelled of disinfectant. Beyond the bars of the cell, that I hoped was temporary, the precinct's yellowish wall was a few inches away. If I pressed against the bars, I could see, to the left, a piece of a desk and unoccupied chair. The shift officer seemed bored, and now and then passed through the room whistling a popular tune. Her uniform seemed about two sizes smaller than she needed, and looked ready to burst under the pressure of her bulges.

"Excuse me, but there's been a misunderstanding," I ventured for the umpteenth time without the slightest hope. "See, I'm a private investigator and I demand an explanation. I have rights, fuck!" I spewed out sounding rotten and inappropriate.

The woman paid not the slightest attention.

Finally, the door opened. Two men with a slightly more pleasant attitude, or at least less indifferent, got me out of the cell and led me through an endless hallway to a small room. Relax, just a formality. In the room, equipped for the effect, they took the inevitable mug shots, with that little black sign familiar from countless flicks. It goes without saying that I valued very little the moment's association with daring films. Face front, left profile, right profile. Undoubtedly I looked hopeless, given the way I was dressed and my foul mood. It was beyond a joke. Bent out of shape by the ritual, I demanded to see a superior.

"Calm down, dear."

"Why should I calm down? This is an outrage. And the dear must be you!" Etcetera, etcetera.

Back at my cell, they allow me to sit at the desk. The bloodhounds take off and I'm alone with the pudgy cop. We continue ignoring each other.

"Do you have a pen?" I venture to ask without conviction.

To my surprise, she offers me a blue ballpoint that she kept in the pocket of her snug shirt.

I don't thank her.

A half hour of solitude went by and I drum on the mistreated desk when the door opens again and a small, stout man walks in.

"Good evening. I'm captain Peña, from narcotics, and this is Wild, my assistant. How are you doing?"

"Well, what can I say…?"

Lost in thought with the juicy graffiti on the desk, mostly in Spanish, I could pretty much care less whatever the new duo had to add. I'd begun doodling and conjecturing on the rude and enigmatic phrases of my predecessors. By some inscrutable coincidence, in style and tone they seemed like what you'd usually find etched into latrine doors, like "Pedro, you're an asshole, but I love you," "*Virjensita mia*, give me courage in these bad times," "Life is long and hard, so suck on life," "I'm gonna slice you up for my mother, slice you up." There was no lack either of the popular iconography of erect penises next to broken hearts and outlines of the Virgin. But probably half of what's mentioned here I've just made up, due to my unfortunate state of consciousness at the time.

"Apologies for the treatment but it was obligatory. We needed to check your credentials. So, you're investigating the Martínez case?" Peña asked me fawningly. I pulled myself together.

"Well, yes, and there's not much I understand." This could get interesting. "Maybe you guys could give me some information."

"That depends."

"On what?"

"Let's just say it depends…" He looked at the assistant, who remained immutable. The assistant had an ungainly manner. He was tall, very thin, and had a tangled matt of reddish hair. I amused myself thinking that he needed only a bowler hat, or looked like Van Gogh but with an extra ear…

"Let's see," I charged ahead, "Martínez was arrested a few years back. Why?"

"As a red."

"And what's that got to do with narcotics?"

"You know about commies, bad folk. Besides, a little while ago we found heroin in Martínez' apartment and some connections overseas."

"Personal use?"

"Too much quantity. And besides, Martínez didn't shoot up."

"Maybe for a friend," I thought out loud, thinking inevitably of Chan Li.

"Who, for example?" Peña's eyes lit up suddenly and his rail mustache moistened almost imperceptibly.

"Well, I'm not sure, he must have some friend addicted to heroin."

"I think you know more than you're telling. You'd be well advised to inform us about your inquiries. It would be more prudent." The cop seemed disappointed in my answer and recovered his bored, official tone.

"And if I don't, then what?"

"Nothing, just be careful. People around here don't like nosey strangers."

"Look, don't threaten me. I'll tell you what I know: in the Miroir bar there is a hidden room with porn and drugs."

"We've known about that for some time. What else."

"Nothing else."

"Loosen your tongue, kid. You know, smarty-pants little girls really bug me." The skinny cop said this in a mellifluous voice, completely out of sorts with his threat. I had to laugh. It seemed more and more like a parody.

"And I don't like jerk-offs who try to act tough," I let out in a roar, more out of curiosity to see how he'd react than truly in anger. The skinny cop's face turned crimson and he lunged at me. Peña stopped him.

The other was turning bright red. Fortunately, someone knocked on the door and the honey-voiced cop reluctantly allowed into the room a pretty woman with straight hair, jacket, and a miniskirt. The Chair of the Department of Romance Languages had come looking for me. The coppers signaled that I could go.

Before leaving, I fired, "And stop putting someone hot on my heals. Spies are what bug me. As far as my arrest, you'll be hearing from my lawyer very soon."

They looked at me curiously, stepping to the side in a mirrored movement to let us pass by.

On the way out, I obtained my revolver and other belongings from the front desk of the station, signed the receipt, and left. At my side, the professor followed without saying a word.

Once in her red-hot sports car, the boss looked at me with a glimmer of pity that left me irritated. For my part, I noticed that her pupils looked dilated. She seemed tired and distant. "Exams," she said. She got out a tissue from her handbag and blew her nose. "I don't feel very good either," she argued, unconvincingly.

"Can you give me something?" I said suddenly.

"Something like what?"

"Well, something. Whatever. I've had a shitty day and I still have the whole night ahead of me."

"Well, I'm really not sure what you're talking about," she began to get nervous.

"Hey, come on, don't play around."

I grabbed her purse, dumped its contents in my lap and went through the professor's private stash. And she'd risked taking the stuff into the station. She must be super stoned.

"Who gives you the drugs?"

"Listen, you better stay out of that."

"Is there anyone else at the University mixed up in this?"

"This is a pretty boring place. I've been here for ten years. I'm sure someone else besides me must be into something."

"Yeah."

I picked out an aromatic piece of hash and began to crumble it into the palm of my hand. Pretty soon I had a nice joint in my lips that I inhaled and moistened with vehemence. Delicious. I passed it over to the poetry professor who did the honors. Parked on official property, we smoked in perfect silence.

With a few hours still remaining until the night's meeting, I decided to take a cold shower and watch the rest of the videos that the deceased had been watching in the days before his death. The movies showed the same sensuality, the same pseudo-communist ideology, and the usual play of light and garish colors of Almodóvar's ambiguous characters. Nothing stood out; maybe it was just a private obsession of old Martínez, who to a certain point was also ambiguous. In one of the urban scenes of the cineaste from La Mancha I notice a familiar detail. I rewind and freeze the scene. Placing a paper over the screen, I trace the outline of a rough drawing.

It was a night crammed with stars. I pressed my pistol tight against my body, as if reminding myself of its presence, which in the end was little reassuring. The meeting place was the alley behind the Miroir.

I waited for a few minutes smoking a cigarette in the cool night that foretold the coming summer. I recalled similar moments in various places, moments of meditation and fatigue. I inhale and exhale the smoke with delight strained with tension. Maybe all would be determined tonight, maybe tomorrow morning I'd be able to leave this tiny place where good intentions and alliances with moral or political taboos you might pay for with your life. Or maybe Martínez had really used Chan Li for his own interests, though I found that hard to believe… The Miroir's guardian, maybe…

A metallic sound resonates behind my back. I whirl around and find myself confronted by a tall figure shadowed by the bright glare of a street lamp. The size, I figure, matches the person who last night had penetrated Chan Lin. A distorted, guttural voice tells me to drop the case, to forget Chan Li, that she was his and that neither the University nor the professor could steal her away.

"That's why you killed the professor? Because he wanted to be free of you and to free Chan Li as well?" I ventured, without knowing exactly what I was suggesting.

I note misgiving in his immediate threat. Reflexively I grip the weapon in my pocket. A glimmer in the night flashes on the blade of an enormous knife. I quickly consider my options and jump to the side, purposely avoiding using my gun. But before I can put into my practice my sophistry, a brutal blow reduces the figure into a dark mound at my feet. Something falls that clangs on the pavement with the revolving sound of a baseball bat. The sound echoes in the night, repeating and sharp, devoid of all murmurs. While reality wakes from its brief lethargy, I notice in front of me the presence of Chan Li, visibly relaxed, as if she'd returned from a long voyage of dependence and anguish. She looks at me as if in complicity. I held her gaze for a moment and that's when I began to understand everything with an unbroken clarity.

A guy ambling through the area notices the strange scene, unleashes a couple of swear words, and I yell to him to call an ambulance and the police. Then I quickly go through Michael Keith's pockets. I find a dozen little bindles as well as a folded page, with a poem in the same handwriting that I'd seen reproduced in other notes and documents. While I adjust the handcuffs on Miguel, I note the approaching lights of the patrol car. No desire to see them. I leave Chan Li next to the unconscious figure of her murderous lover and return to my room convincing myself that Li's future will sew itself up fine.

On the way home, I unfold Martínez' poem:

Sliding down the perfect
vertex of your spine
Through the undulating angle
of my decrepitude
I can barely modulate you without hurting myself

My dear love pierced
by wire and metal
metal that penetrates you while I remain
exhausted by my contemplation
of my total absence
  of you.

Old Martínez in love, the professor devoted to philanthropies and century-end metaphors of perversion and insanity. Perhaps the perfect combination for this remote and empty part of the United States. Maybe the price for the contradiction was his death and an obscene inscription in his left buttock, a design as rash and savage as the texts in urinals and writing desks, graphic labyrinths of anxiety and passion.

Back in my room, I call the police and prepare a detailed report while the television flashes the scrambled images of a pornographic cable channel to which the owner of the apartment evidently wasn't subscribed. In the distortion, men and women humping, hermaphroditic creatures moaning in surreal undulations.

I call Pedro. Before I can say anything he warns me about the complete lack of interest at the company that had hired me. I ask him if he wants to know the result of my investigation and he seems indifferent.

"Someone in the department?" he asks. "Maybe the Chair? She's always seemed a little kinky... Or possibly someone from the Miroir?"

"You're always right on, Pedro. Actually no, not the Chair, let alone someone from the Miroir; after all, you need an ID and authorization to enter the language lab. In the end, it was a fairly common crime of passion. During his stay in China, Martínez had gotten to know Chan Li and had begun the long and complicated process permitting the bright Spanish student to attend doctoral courses in Midwest College. The Tiananmen Square incident, in which Martínez participated in, had sped up the process. Li's boyfriend had been killed in the incident, and Chan Li would have ended up the same if not for the efforts of professor Martínez and the University's discrete collaboration in getting her out of China immediately. In that regard they'd prepared a document that affirmed that Chan Li hadn't participated in the sit in, and that helped her to get out of the country. On the other hand, while these types of arrangements were undoubtedly common in the period following the massacre, the manager of the office of International Studies preferred that I not investigate those kinds of procedures."

"And then?"

"Miguel has been devoted to Martínez for a long time, I didn't realize at first, and that was one of the reasons why he continued to study there for so long, to be close to Martínez. But Martínez always kept himself aloof, professional prudence maybe. When Chan Li arrived and Miguel sensed she was taking over his territory, he took revenge precisely by loving her with absolute devotion, and indirectly by involving her in drugs."

"How did that happen?"

"Miguel was the town's heroin dealer, and he'd gone into it with the Miroir folks, porno spectacle and everything. No doubt he planted the heroin in Martínez' house to complicate his life. When Martínez was charged and he learned about Miguel's scene, he probably got furious and convened a meeting in the Miroir the night of the murder. Martínez threatened to denounce Miguel and the latter decided to kill him. Anyway, Miguel had been worried about Martínez for some time. Miguel knew Martínez' help toward Chan Li had been crucial to her career. Her dissertation was almost done and she was likely to find work somewhere in the United States. As far as the drawing, Miguel seems to have copied it from a graffiti in one of the movies from Martínez repertoire, a copy of which is in his apartment."

"And what will happen to Chan Li?"

"The girl had been a bit aimless, brought on possibly by alienation and bitterness. I don't think she's gotten over the death of her friends, and her feeling of frustration and loss after the massacre in Beijing. She probably feels bewildered and hopeless, especially after Martínez' murder. With Martínez dead, not only her moral support but at least her immediate option to leave the university died as well, a contingency that was convenient for the desperate Miguel, who had been noticing the gradual detachment of Chan Li. Miguel probably also knows that Chan Li is applying on her own for a green card, paradoxically with the help of the Chinese government, which has been making these things easier since the massacre."

"Wow, how morbid! So everyone in that lost town has a double life."

"What can I say? Definitely, what you call a 'double life' isn't just an urban prerogative. Not only the professor, but the girl and her boyfriend had double lives. The first tried to redeem the second, or vice versa. Anyway, in the pit of heroin into which Chan Li had descended there were other levels of dependence. The professor wanted to help her at the same time he helped himself. And Mike couldn't accept that the girl might escape from his own obsession."

I hang up the telephone and take from my pocket the poem that the tormented professor had written, looking at the other side. The metaphors of his work, of the apocalypse of the century's end, remained in the distorted drawing of an erect penis painfully penetrated by a syringe.

End

Translated from the Spanish by John W. Warren

Asesinato en el
laboratorio de idiomas

El cuerpo había aparecido degollado en el laboratorio de idiomas, entre las cabinas doce y trece, con un dibujo obsceno en la nalga izquierda. El tosco dibujo consistía en un pene en erección atravesado por una jeringa. Las especulaciones abordaron la estrafalaria posibilidad de una venganza feminista: un grupo extremista antisistema blandiendo jeringas contra las nalgas homofóbicas del profesorado de español. Mientras los reporteros multiplicaban fotografías y comentarios extravagantes, me acerqué discretamente al encargado del laboratorio, un hombre pequeñito y medio calvo que me miraba desconfiado mientras le preguntaba datos sobre el difunto.

No conocía bien al finado, pero le había visto en varias ocasiones hurgando entre los cassettes de italiano y el material audiovisual. A veces se quedaba horas en las pequeñas cabinas con la mirada fija en las imágenes subtituladas. No parecía tener gustos especiales en su elección. La noche del asesinato se había decidido por una película china subvencionada por el Ministerio de Cultura del país, que hacía una apología solapada del gobierno comunista. Ese tipo de películas y las de Almodóvar parecían dominar la lista de la selección que el difunto, el profesor Martínez, había devorado en los últimos dos meses.

Augusto Javier Martínez, profesor de literatura decimonónica del Midwest College, era oriundo de un pueblecito de Guadalajara. Agobiado por unos padres abusivos y las limitaciones culturales, Martínez decidió solicitar una beca de intercambio que una entidad bancaria facilitaba con una Universidad del Sur de los Estados Unidos. La posibilidad le había siempre fascinado. América tenía el esplendor de las películas de John Wayne y el perfume exuberante de la no menos Marilyn. La Marylin, mito de los cincuenta que dominaba su imaginación y la pared blanca de su ordenado apartamento.

La cocinera, señora María Smith, no conocía los hábitos del profesor, pero siempre le pareció sospechoso por un instinto innato a la desconfianza. El pobresito profésor Martines, siempre en su casa, frente al *computer*. Señor muy listo y reservado, había algo raro en él. Aquella mañana había chequeado su *mail* y parecía más raro de lo normal.

Hurgando en la papelera recuperé una nota a la que la policía local, chapucera ella, no había prestado atención. Pub Miroir, Pine 142. Y allí fui, a las 8:00 de la tarde, esperando sacar algo en claro de todo aquel enredo en que mi amigo Pedro me había metido.

Hacía tiempo que me había alejado de la investigación privada por motivos que no vienen a cuento. Ahora estaba decidida a reempezar una vida académica que había abandonado harta de la política asfixiante de los varios departamentos que intenté. La muerte del profesor Martínez me interesaba por lo que había en común con mis propias frustraciones. Yo también había nacido en un pueblecito de provincias de España, creciendo en un barrio marginal de Madrid donde mis padres se habían instalado de por vida. Allí, en Madrid, es donde había ejercido la investigación privada más por solaz que por las magras y poco consistentes remuneraciones. Me fascinaba la sordidez de los encuentros y desencuentros pasionales. Disfrutaba la sensación del riesgo entre vomitonas de los barrios bajos o los perfumes de las damas que aparecían en la revistas de moda. Pero aquello se acabó desde que vine a USA escapando de mis propios fantasmas, como todos los que venimos a este paraíso inclasificable.

Así que, en realidad, mi buen amigo Pedro no tuvo que insistir mucho en que me encargara del caso. La entidad para la que trabajaba Pedro, una empresa editorial de índole tanto religiosa como sensacionalista en la que también había participado el propio Martínez, me había ofrecido una suma nada despreciable como anticipo de los derechos del morboso mercado al que servía. Tenían especial interés en que una persona próxima al contexto académico diera luz sobre un caso turbio que la policía local chapotearía hasta poderlo dar por cerrado si no se producía otro incidente. Por su parte, la universidad, pequeñísimo colegio de provincias, haría lo posible por enterrar el bochornoso suceso, ignorándolo tan pronto como fuera superado el escándalo del momento. Como sucedió que yo estaba merodeando por zonas próximas al Midwest College, bastaron apenas un par de horas para presentarme frente al cuerpo del delito.

Miroir era un bareto adyacente a la calle principal y única arteria de aquel mal llamado pueblo. Me puse junto a la ventana a ver pasar los coches grandotes y los camiones destartalados que avanzaban pesadamente de un extremo al otro de la calle-pueblo. Desde aquella posición podía observar los límites del mismo. Más allá de ambos extremos de la carretera no había absolutamente nada. El horizonte azul dividido en pentagramas telegráficos se repetía a sí mismo hasta el infinito. Cómo podía cometerse un crimen en ese contexto estéril era algo que parecía insólito, o perfectamente lógico, según se mire.

Hacia las 8:30 entró un señor atocinado con gorra de béisbol de los Yankees que se sentó en la barra. La camarera, alta, de rasgos orientales y fuerte acento, le ofreció familiarmente un vaso de cerveza que el grasiento señor engulló al instante. Los pantalones apenas lograban cubrir las pesadas nalgas, por lo que el gigante tenía que subírselos a cada rato con un gesto brusco. Miró hacia mi mesa y me sonrío al tiempo que soltaba un eructo. Sonreí a mi vez, fingiendo coquetería cervecera, de puta barata. Se acercó masticando un «puedo sentarme, muñeca» y con un movimiento pesado se sentó la mole bloqueando una sección de la calle.

Me inventé inmigrante del sur al tiempo que el monstruo, George Puckey, me contaba su no-historia. Finalmente, pude llevar la rústica conversación a su cotidianidad en el bar Miroir. Me dijo que allí había marcha, y me hizo un guiño. Me señaló con un índice grueso y manchado de grasa una puerta que, de no ser indicada, pasaría totalmente desapercibida. Acepté acompañarle a la puerta con mis sensores alerta por si las moscas. Dentro, en la penumbra, una barra de bar, copia fiel de la que habíamos dejado, permanecía en la oscuridad y en un silencio de animal en reposo. Fingí no comprender el propósito de aquel otro bar al tiempo que la mole empezaba a tocar mi trasero. Me insinuó que allí había, ciertas noches, intercambios ilegales: putas, drogas, maricones, mariguana, María que rica estás. Bofetón. Antes de irme, ostentando indignación le doy mi teléfono porque, a pesar del descaro, me gustó el mozote, y no estaría mal fumarnos un porro en el otro lado del bar de la calle Pine. Entre desconcertado y satisfecho, el animal me entregó una sonrisa imperfecta y amarilla sin quitar los ojos de mis tetas. Vale guapa, me gustan difíciles.

Tenía dos horas antes de que cerraran el laboratorio audiovisual que había sido finalmente rescatado a la curiosidad del público, sin rastro ya de cadáver. Empecé a ingerir las mismas películas del atracón del profe muerto. Auriculares, moviola, y una joven que aparece y desaparece en sus cuitas político-amorosas de de la China pre-revolucionaria. La muchacha con sus ansias libertarias en una sociedad que la oprime como mujer y como individuo. Y esos primeros planos, tipo Hollywood, de una boca carnosa y de un cuerpo mórbido carente del estereotipo frágil de la mujer oriental.

Almodóvar resultón, paródico, tomándonos el pelo a todo español que presuma de tal. Edulcorado con colores horteras: ahora una peluca, ahora un juego de intercambio de sexos donde menos te lo esperas. Y ese cuerpo de Bibí Andersen que recarga modulaciones de luz.

Me llevo el resto de las cintas al apartamento que Pedro me ha facilitado. Sigo hipnotizada por el despliegue de formas y colores hasta más allá de las cinco de la mañana. Cuatro horas más tarde, desayuno con la jefe del departamento de Lenguas Romances.

Croissant, huevos revueltos y zumo de tomate con pimienta y sal. Alicia Jiménez, profesora murciana de literatura peninsular, especialista en mujeres poetas contemporáneas, parece dada a las confesiones.

—No es fácil para una mujer dominar en este mundo de hombres, tú debes de saberlo muy bien. A eso hay que añadir las tensiones tradicionales entre la sección de francés y la de español. (Muerdo al croissant.) Nuestro departamento ha sido dominado por los de francés sistemáticamente, en contra de la realidad social del país en que claramente domina el español. Parece una conspiración del sistema para anular el tremendo potencial y la historia de nuestra cultura... Finalmente..., me dieron a mí la posición de jefa quizás sólo porque soy española, ¿te puedes creer? (pausa dramática), sólo porque represento, en este juego de estereotipos, los símbolos del imperialismo y demás. Una mierda en verdad.

—Pero quizás ahora tienes el poder de modificar esos estereotipos. ¿No? —La tuteo, animada por su iniciativa, a la que estoy por lo demás acostumbrada seguramente porque mi aspecto pequeño y gordete invita al tuteo y hasta a la palmadita de suficiencia.

La doctora Alicia Jiménez es alta, lleva grueso maquillaje y unas bolsitas azules bajo los ojos que hacen pensar en noches de insomnio. Viste con un aire que aquí suele calificarse de «europeo», es decir, no identificable con la imagen habitual de muchas de las mujeres del Midwest americano: pelo esculpido semipermanentado, vaqueros de diario, flores y encajes en los cuellos los domingos. La doctora Jiménez, por el contrario, lleva pantalones de pinza y una blusa gris que deja transparentar, muy levemente, el sujetador blanco. Después de una discusión sobre las poetas postnovísimas, me habla finalmente de Martínez.

—Curioso personaje. Era muy reservado fuera y dentro del departamento. Apenas participaba de las actividades sociales que organizamos. Por ejemplo, todos los primeros viernes del mes tenemos un... gathering social, quiero decir, una fiestecilla en la que nos tomamos un vino con queso y a la que están invitados los pocos estudiantes graduados que tenemos. Ahora que recuerdo, de las dos o tres veces que Martínez vino a las charlas, una fue el viernes pasado.

—¿Quién más vino a la fiesta?

—Los de costumbre. Mario, especialista en colonial. Skilling, medievalista. Su mujer, Susana, medievalista también. Philippe, James y Mary de francés... Te paso una lista si quieres.

—¿Quienes vinieron entre los estudiantes graduados?

—Miguel, quiero decir, Michael Keith, es uno de nuestros habituales. Chico dinámico pero un poco ligero de cascos. Lleva aquí más años que el obispo, quiero decir, que el doctor Johnson. Y no sé, no conozco los nombres de los estudiantes de francés... Pero también vino el viernes pasado la novia de Miguel, Chan Li. Cosa rara, porque la chica es tan tímida que apenas se atreve con la hipocresía de nuestra pedante conversación... En realidad, la fiesta es exclusivamente para nosotros y nuestros delicados egos e, inconscientemente, excluimos a los estudiantes graduados en cuyo entusiasmo reconocemos nuestro propio idealismo fracasado... Nosotros, profesores en un lugar perdido, a pesar de nuestra pedantería, sabemos que apenas somos dinosaurios de película B.

Antes de que se dispersara en su afligida elucubración quise bajarla a la mesa del comedor universitario donde mi segunda taza de café aguado se había quedado fría.

—Esa Chan Li. ¿Era estudiante de español o de francés?

—De español. Y, por cierto, estaba haciendo su tesis con Martínez. No sé que va a hacer ahora, la pobre. A estas alturas, y con el MLA encima.

—¿Dónde vive la chica?

—En el dormitorio de mujeres. Aquí son tan puritanos que tienen dormitorios separados para chicos y para chicas. A las 11 de la noche toda persona del sexo opuesto debe desalojar el dormitorio respectivo. Ridículo. Lo curioso del caso es que, efectivamente, el número de embarazos entre las estudiantes se ha reducido considerablemente a partir de la aplicación de esa regla. La ansiedad paternalista no puede, al fin y al cabo, ignorar la promiscuidad sexual de estos críos que a pesar de la falsa libertad siguen extraprotegidos. Apenas les dejan crecer...

Antes de salir bebí con asco el resto de mi café y añadí un par de dólares a la generosa propina. «No se preocupe», insistió la jefa haciendo un gesto cómplice; «también la propina la pone el departamento», añadió.

Chan Li compartía el cuarto con una anglosajona voluminosa que se movía con una agilidad que contradecía su peso. Li ocupaba la parte inferior del cuarto, que tenía una apariencia simple y meticulosamente ordenada, llena de algunos objetos esenciales delicados y convencionales. En la parte de arriba, sobre un loft o entramado de madera, se disimulaba el desorden de la anglosajona. El cuarto olía a estofado de lata que, sin duda, la segunda acababa de preparar en un hornillo para el efecto, y en contra de las restricciones del dormitorio que no permitían cocinar en los cuartos. Después de disculparse por un tremendo eructo que me recordó a George, Shanon me comunicó que Chan Li seguramente estaría con Michael en la sala de ordenadores de la biblioteca porque mañana era la fecha límite para solicitar una importante beca que Li quería obtener. Y hacia allí mi dirigí.

La primavera sentaba de maravilla a los chicos y chicas que exhibían sus sonrisas de anuncio publicitario con solidaria arrogancia. Los movimientos eran suaves o precipitados, dependiendo de los apretados horarios de los estudiantes. Entre bicicletas y saludos neutros, llegué a la mole de la biblioteca, que se distinguía por un aburrido estilo rectangular y unas amplias escaleras en las que algunos mozos y mozas se estiraban al sol. Después de pelearme con el personal de la entrada que literalmente radiografió mi morena presencia en aquellas instalaciones del saber, alcancé la sala de ordenadores situada en la planta quinta.

Fue fácil reconocerlos en aquella amplia sala repleta de gorras de béisbol cuyos portadores se afanaban en aporrear las teclas del ordenador. Unas horas más y la tortura del trabajo acabaría y casi todos, gorras en ristre, podrían disfrutar de la merecida cerveza del viernes por la tarde. Por supuesto, prácticamente ninguno tenía los veintiún años exigidos para el consumo de alcohol.

Chan Li depositó su mirada sobre mí a medida que me acercaba. Tenía rasgos redondos y ojos abultados. Su tez era morena y sus labios gruesos y sensuales. Mike-Miguel acariciaba en movimientos verticales la espalda de la chica con la mirada fija en la pantalla de fondo azul del ordenador, completamente abstraído. Era la última sección de la pesada solicitud. Entre los impresos oficiales esparcidos por la mesa adyacente pude advertir la firma del director de tesis, Dr. Martínez.

Me presenté como candidata a estudiante graduada de español y les indiqué que quería saber su honesta opinión sobre el departamento. Miguel tomó la voz cantante de inmediato.

—Verás, éste es un departamento pequeño, hay pocos especialistas interesantes. ¿Qué campo te interesa?

—No estoy muy segura todavía. Me interesa el periodo moderno, principalmente la cultura finisecular —aventuré a decir. Sabía que Martínez trabajaba en el XIX, pero todavía no había tenido ocasión de rastrear su investigación más reciente.

—¡Qué coincidencia! Precisamente Li está pidiendo una beca basada en su investigación sobre el fin de siglo.

—Me encantaría conocer ese proyecto.

Li pareció dudar un momento, y al final se decidió.

—Mi trabajo conecta el fin del siglo XIX con el fin del siglo XX. La situación de crisis, las metáforas epidémicas de origen sexual como la sífilis o el AIDS respectivamente...

—SIDA —corrigió Mike-Miguel. Parece que la muchacha no apreció la interrupción.

—El SIDA —corrigió Chan Li—. Creo que es un tema con mucho potencial.

—¿Se trata de tu tesis? —aventuré.

—Sí —respondió, y pareció oscurecerse un poco su mirada.

—¿Cómo vas con la tesis? —insistí.

Parecía un poco infeliz ante la pregunta y Mike se decidió por ella:

—Ahora está estancada, necesita cambiar de director de tesis pero, como te dijimos, hay pocos especialistas en el departamento. Su ex director era un fenómeno en ese campo. Estaba como una chota pero tenía mucho talento, todo hay que decirlo, ¡joder! Al muy cabrón se le caía la baba con la Li. El pobre iba super quemao, pero a mí siempre me pareció un poco marica. ¡Coño!

Mike se enorgullecía de su desparpajo español aprendido admirablemente en una larga visita escolar a España. Para enfatizar su dominio solía adornar su verborrea con tacos que no venían a cuento. Li parecía un poco desorientada. Finalmente, se decidió a hablar otra vez, desviándose del terreno que había abordado su amigo.

—Quizás cambie el tema. Sé que a estas alturas no es muy inteligente, pero me siento incómoda ahora después de... Tengo que presentarme al MLA en diciembre y he de tomar una decisión. De momento, creo que es útil procurar conseguir cierta seguridad con esta aplicación para el gobierno.

—Me parece muy bien —asentí.

Llegué a casa definitivamente agotada. En el contestador una luz parpadeaba indicando tres mensajes. El primero era de Pedro. Que cómo iba, que llamaría más tarde. El segundo de George, invitándome, creo, a una cita esa misma noche. Tuve que rebobinar el mensaje tres veces para poder entenderlo. El tercer mensaje fue sólo un silencio largo. Evidentemente, la persona que llamó no quiso ni colgar ni hablar, procurando con ello imponer cierta inquietud. A punto de echarme un rato en la cama, suena el teléfono. Tardo un momento en decidirme a coger el auricular. En el otro lado de la línea telefónica, el saludo inconfundible de Pedro.

—Hey chica, ¿cómo estás? No hay manera de pillarte. ¿Cómo va todo?

—A medias, pero necesito que me des alguna información.

—Lo que quieras. Pero antes tengo que darte malas noticias. La empresa que me pidió contratarte ha cambiado de opinión en su interés por el caso Martínez. Parece que se empiezan a interesar por otro suceso que ha ocurrido en el este del país y que podría dar suculentos beneficios a su sección sensacionalista. Una mujer que castró a su marido... Un tinglado. Pero dime.

—Mientras que me paguen... Oye, me tienes que decir a qué se dedicaba el finado recientemente y qué hacía para tu editorial.

—Martínez se había interesado recientemente por la teoría sociosexual, o algo así, del fin de siglo pasado. Crisis, enfermedades venéreas, decadentismo, etc. En la editorial tenía ocasionalmente una columna pseudo-filosófica donde mezclaba comentarios de crímenes pasionales y teoría del cine. Si quieres te los paso.

—Un tío un poco raro.

—Era un buenazo. Pero algo pirado. Tenía ideas de cambiar el mundo y regenerar a los jóvenes... Ah, también escribía poemas.

—¿Poemas?

—Sí, eran tan raros y oscuros como su prosa.

—¿Cómo era su vida amorosa?

—De lo más secreta. No se le ha conocido pareja de ningún tipo, y se especula sobre su orientación sexual.

—Ya veo... ¿Cómo te va el sabático?

—De puta madre, pero, como ves, me pierdo lo más suculento.

—Te has librado, diría yo. Bueno mira, que esto, desde Florida, te va a costar un huevo.

—Paga la empresa. Llamada profesional, ya sabes...

—Sí, sí. Ya sé. Pues nada, hasta pronto. Pásalo bien.

—Hasta pronto, y date prisa con el caso que estos son como veletas. Suerte, guapa.

—Chao.

Las 9:00 de la noche y viernes. Busqué en mi maleta lo más hortera que pude encontrar. Cargué el maquillaje. Insistí sin apenas darme cuenta en la línea sobre los ojos, dando un cierto efecto de rasgado. Rojo carmín en los labios y mucho colorete. Rojo y negro, estupendo.

Faltaba media hora para la cita con George pero quise tantear antes el terreno por mi cuenta. Me senté en la misma mesa del Miroir, pudiendo comprobar desde allí la discreta actividad en la puerta escondida. La camarera, de aspecto oriental, me miraba ocasionalmente. Noté en ella cierto aire de disgusto. Desapareció para ser sustituida por un hombre de movimientos lánguidos y enorme bigote. El bar parecía tener un aire distinto, algo diferente que intuía especular. Opuesto al bar del otro lado, tras la puerta escondida, el bar donde yo me encontraba: jóvenes con gorra atiborrándose a cerveza; muchachas en tejanos con camiseta ajustada y bambas blanquísimas, gozando el ritual de los viernes. La verdad es que mi facha desentonaba bastante. Frente a mi caña larga de cerveza, espero.

George llegó veinte minutos tarde. Vino a la mesa y me quiso dar un morreo que desvié hacia el vaso de cerveza. Le hizo gracia el gesto y soltó una carcajada. Me tomó del brazo y nos dirigimos a la puerta clandestina.

—¡Ella no! —determinó la camarera, quien controlaba ahora el acceso al recinto. Definitivamente yo no le gustaba.

—Ella entra porque me sale da los huevos —creo que dijo el salvaje de George, lanzando una especie de amortiguado berrido empapado de alcohol en el rostro de la mujer. Imperturbable, la guardiana se compuso su descolocado mechón de pelo, se hizo a un lado y, lanzándome una mirada despreciativa, nos dejó pasar.

Tras la puerta empezaba lo que parecía un striptease. Una mujer joven apareció en la oscuridad del escenario matizada por un débil rayo de luz. Vestía pedazos de cuero negro enlazados con cintas y hebillas que pretendían dar agresividad a su cuerpo diminuto, casi púber. Iba avanzando en su baile con movimientos levemente obscenos y ondulaciones que interrumpían el haz luminoso. Desde el sitio donde me encontraba apenas podía ver sus ojos, apreciar su rostro del que resaltaban unos labios sobrecargados de rojo carmín. Desató uno de los lazos dejando al desnudo uno de sus blancos, impecables brazos. Repitió la cadencia con el otro brazo y con las piernas. El público empezó a emocionarse y a soltar berridos como los del propio George, o quizás era el berrido de George repetido en los ecos de espejo de la oscuridad.

Cuando empezó a acariciar sus pequeños senos, la mano fina de la musa alcanzó el vértice del lazo del corpiño. Se detuvo en cada cadencia del desenlace, del desnudo paulatino. Cuando parecía finalizar con su torso, sus manos permanecieron sobre el resto de material a que se había reducido el corpiño de cuero, ocultándose así los senos. Mientras tanto, los labios se humedecían con una lengua-molusco flexible y perfectamente cómplice.

De espaldas a la oscuridad del público, se deshace del corpiño sosteniéndolo con la mano derecha, extendida, como sus piernas abiertas y tensas. Rotación de culo en abierta circunferencia que sostiene en la posición hacia un público entre hechizado y animalizado con el espectáculo decididamente seductor. Fascinada a mi vez, procuro concentrarme en poder verle la cara a la chica.

Cuando parecía que iba a concluir el strip-tease, sale al escenario una segunda figura indefinible, inclasificable. La muchacha sigue de espaldas al público en su posición axial. El otro personaje se le acerca y empieza a acariciarla, primero con la mano, visiblemente, operando como la imaginación del excitado público. De inmediato se coloca detrás de la muchacha y empieza a recorrerla con la lengua empezando por la nuca, después de separar el negro y lacio cabello, y siguiendo por la espalda hasta el culo y hasta el sexo todavía amordazado de cuero negro y brillante. Se detiene, en cuclillas, con la lengua en el sexo de ella, la cual parece gozarla con sus rítmicos movimientos que acompaña con pequeños gemidos de placer.

¡El no va más! Los americanos se suben por las paredes de sus mentes sobrecalentadas y mi George que me toca el culo sin reserva alguna.

La figura lamedora exhibe también un cabello largo y lacio, pero es alta, mucho más alta que la muchacha. Finalmente, la persona alta, de forma suave, delicadamente, quita la última prenda al cuerpo púber mediante el mismo registro de desenlace. Desprendida de ella, la muchacha exhibe su culito blanco y se deja hacer por la persona que, poniéndola de perfil para mayor efecto, la empieza insospechadamente a sodomizar con perfecta armonía de la música, la misma música que sirvió de preámbulo a la escena sexual, hipnótica. Mantienen ambos el ritmo que progresivamente se intensifica, se intensifica, hasta el supuesto clímax maravillosamente unánime que coincide, cómo no, con el crescendo de la música.

Aparentemente exhaustos los dos, la muchacha proyecta su rostro hacia el público y reconozco en su cara los ojos abultados de la estudiante graduada. La música y las luces se apagan desapareciendo los objetos como en el espectáculo irreal de un sueño.

Perpleja por la evidencia, me deshago del mastodonte y me dirijo a lo que creo camerinos. En la puerta de uno de ellos me enfrento otra vez con la guardiana, personaje ubicuo al parecer, que avanza contra mí en actitud amenazante. «Largo o te rajo», me dijo mientras manipulaba el resorte de una navaja que se me antojó enorme. Decido esfumarme con el deje de reconocimiento en la boca. No sólo la estudiante strip-teaser sino la presencia de la otra entidad en el escenario me resulta familiar. Sin embargo, me quedo al acecho en el pliegue de una esquina próxima, y espero. La guardiana enrolla un canuto y empieza a aspirar el humo con deleite. Le envidio el gesto. Al poco rato se vuelve hacia la puerta para abrirla y en el movimiento de la misma reconozco dentro del cuarto la triste escena de la estudiante strip-teaser pinchándose heroína, aparentemente feliz y aliviada, desesperadamente aliviada, en un gesto inefable que se intuye bajo el pesado maquillaje.

Veo una señal roja de EXIT y escapo a la noche de un campus de madrugada que auguraba el fin de semana de paroxismo. Sexo y alcohol falsamente contenidos, éxtasis de cerveza y música rap en cadencias que inevitablemente asocié a aquella otra barra del bar Miroir. Los grupos de muchachos y muchachas se sucedían por las calles, deteniéndose en pórticos de columnas dóricas en los que musculosos cofrades invitaban a la juerga. En silencio, las patrullas azules de los polis del campus vigilan.

Asciendo por el camino de ladrillos rojos que lleva a mi apartamento, procurando con la soledad y la extrañeza en que me colocaban aquellas multitudes felices, ordenar quizás mis ideas. Junto al portal de mi apartamento, un bulto gris me pide una moneda. Rebusco en los bolsillos y le extiendo el suelto. Me da su bendición.

En la sala de estar, el parpadeo de la máquina otra vez. Presiono el botón del contestador que me remite una voz gutural, amenazante, que me invita a a una cita la noche siguiente. Que vaya sola. Me acuesto con la escena de Li pinchándose y su angustiosa dependencia. Todo empezaba a encajar de algún modo, pero no sabía muy bien de qué manera. ¿Y esa voz en el contestador?

Por la mañana intenté localizar a Li pero me resultó imposible. Llamé a Miguel. Quedamos en encontrarnos de inmediato en su dormitorio. Hacía un día resplandeciente y el campus, con muy poco estudiantes por las calles, recuperaba un cierto sabor local. Las familias iban y venían con sus helados y carritos de bebés, mientras los niños corrían felices por el césped. Apenas quedaban ecos de la noche en los pulcros rincones de las calles. Las fraternidades, bestias en reposo, mantenían un inquietante silencio.

El edificio de dormitorios en que se alojaba Miguel consistía en un complejo triangular al que se accedía por una estrecha entrada con barra giratoria. Tuve que identificarme con el carnet de visitante que para el efecto me habían proporcionado y, después de una llamada del vigilante de turno, se presentó saltimbanqui Miguel. Cruzamos una explanada verde donde un consumado optimista jugaba al frisbee con su perro.

Las cabriolas felices del animal parecían la única nota dinámica en aquel plácido recinto que se empeñaba en no despertar. Ya en el cuarto de Miguel, le comento a medias la película de la noche anterior y, sin hacer comentarios directos, el chico pareció desentenderse de todo el asunto. Conocía la dependencia de Li a la heroína pero decía ignorar cualquier otra vinculación ilegal. Era evidente que Miguel adoraba a su novia. Empezó a hablarme del interés que Martínez había mostrado por su novia, alardeando en sus comentarios de un desprecio y sorna que apenas lograban encubrir sus celos. Me dijo también que el profesor Martínez había escrito un poema a la chica que tenía por su cuarto. El muy gilipollas.

—¿Por qué tienes tú ese poema?

Pareció contrariado.

—Bueno, se lo pillé a Li. A ella le da igual. Total, pasaba de los requiebros del viejo, pero lo respetaba mucho. Voy a ver si encuentro el poemita —y desapareció en la habitación colindante, presunta oficina del muchacho.

Mientras esperaba a Miguel, recreé mis ojos en el desconcierto de libros, ropa sucia, carpetas, apuntes y objetos desperdigados por su cuarto. Había también un maletín con frascos de maquillaje y carmín, que atribuí a Chan Li, y también una heterogénea colección de cintas de vídeo que incluía *Terminator*, *Star Trek*, *La muerte de Mikel* y *Laberinto de pasiones*. En casi todas las fotografías que colgaban por las paredes aparecía la sonrisa de la muchacha: Chan Li en una sentada reivindicativa contra el aumento de impuestos de la

Universidad; Chan Li en el equipo femenino de béisbol; Chan Li con Martínez y el propio Miguel en la playa; Chan Li con Miguel en una impresión digital, bastante mala, con fondo de sentada multitudinaria y pancartas en chino. Me intrigó la copia digital. La imagen de Miguel no encajaba demasiado. Bajo el marco de la foto, forzándola apenas, pude ver en el extremo inferior derecho una fecha: 04 JUN 89. Desvío la mirada hacia la Chan Li del béisbol cuando oigo la voz del chico a mis espaldas.

—A que es preciosa —enfatizó Miguel regresando de la habitación—. Aunque no lo parezca, Chan Li es muy fuerte, ella solía ser bate del equipo de la Universidad y era imbatible. Bate imbatible, ¿gracioso, no?

Miguel parecía feliz con su juego de palabras y entre carcajadas un poco fuera de tono me comunicó con forzada indiferencia que no podía encontrar el poema. «Lo tendrá Chan Li», concluyó.

—¿Desde cuándo conoces a Chan Li?

—Pues desde el curso 89-90. Apenas sabía inglés cuando vino pero yo le ayudé con todo. Es muy inteligente. Se maneja muy bien. Nos vamos a casar muy pronto, por lo de la tarjeta verde y todo eso. Y nos vamos a ir de esta mierda de sitio.

—Yo pensaba que te gustaba estar aquí. Llevas muchos años, ¿no?

—Bueno..., sí, unos cuantos. Pero ahora no quiero quedarme más —creo que empezó a ponerse un poquito nervioso. Decidí insistir en el tema.

—¿Y qué va a pasar si Chan Li consigue un trabajo lejos de aquí? Tengo entendido que todavía tú andas muy mal con la tesis...

Era evidente que el comentario no le gustó.

—Oye, eso a ti no te importa —se irritó de pronto y se me puso casi violento—. Además, me tienes harto con tus preguntas.

—Bueno, bueno, tranquilo que ya me voy —adopté una actitud conciliadora. Por el momento no me interesaba revelarle la verdadera razón de mi visita al Midwest College—. Mera curiosidad —concluí—. Si ves a Chan Li, dile que me gustaría hablar con ella.

Miguel no dijo nada.

Me prometí regresar en mejor oportunidad y despidiéndome deprisa me dirigí a la oficina de asuntos internacionales que imaginaba cerrada durante el fin de semana. Así que llamé al responsable y mientras el tal Smith se desplazaba de su casa al campus, aproveché para almorzarme tremendo bocata de embutido con todo tipo de añadidos y salsas. El exceso fue debido al malentendido o, mejor dicho, desencuentro entre la dependienta del local y mi limitado inglés. Casi siempre procuro simplificar, digo a todo yes y que pase lo que pase. Pero esta vez la pasada había sido descomunal: mayonesa, ketchup, mostaza, cebolla, pepinillos en vinagre, pimiento morrón, tomate, lechuga y una sustancia roja que no supe identificar. Todo eso además del embutido, claro. Procurando espantar el fantasma plausible de la indigestión, me comí todo el bocata y llegué ahíta a la puerta de la oficina casi al mismo tiempo que el alto y refinado Mr. Smith. El contraste entre ambos resultaba extremo y aquello me hizo sentir un tanto insegura. El pepinillo se me empezaba a repetir. Procuré componerme como pude.

—Encantada.

—Encantado. Por favor, pase... Tome asiento —me ofreció con fría ceremonia—. Me han dicho que le facilite la información que desee. Usted me dirá en qué puedo servirla.

—Quisiera acceder al fichero de Chan Li.

Puso gesto de sorpresa.

—Creía que estaba investigando el lamentable... «suceso» de Martínez. No sé qué puede tener que ver eso con Li.

—Veo que tiene un trato muy familiar con ella.

—Conocemos bien a nuestros estudiantes extranjeros. Chan Li es, por otra parte, un caso especial —me concedió y de inmediato pareció arrepentirse. Esperó mi reacción.

—¿Y eso?

—La información es siempre confidencial.

Era evidente que a pesar de su afirmación primera, Mr. Smith se resistía a cooperar.

—Le recuerdo que estoy investigando un caso de homicidio y si no colabora me veré obligada a informar de ello —la parquedad y reticencia de mi interlocutor empezaba a fastidiarme.

Algo incomodado, el hombre se levantó de su silla y se dirigió hacia el enorme archivador de metal que estaba a mi espalda. Pretendiendo empolvar mi nariz, detalle inverosímil para el que me conozca pero pertinente al caso, miré reflejada en el espejo de la polvera la esbelta figura del señor buceando entre papeles. Pareció localizar una carpeta amarilla de la cual sustrajo unos cuantos folios. Cerró ruidosamente el archivador y guardé a mi vez el espejito. Por encima de mi hombro, Mr. Smith empezó a distribuir los papeles frente a mí a medida que enumeraba. Del oscuro traje emanaba un residuo de aroma que inevitablemente asocié a esos perfumes de moda que usan los adolescentes.

—Aquí está la solicitud de beca para estudiar español. La aceptación de entrada al país. Fotocopias de sus documentos. Todo en orden.

—Tengo entendido que los estudiantes que vienen de países como China precisan de algún tipo de autorización o contrato por parte del gobierno... Yo no veo ningún formulario por aquí.

— ... Es evidente que si tenemos todos los datos de inmigración en orden, también lo estarían en su momento los papeles a los que se refiere... Por lo demás, no tiene mayor relevancia el asunto —el señor Smith seguía condescendiente y evasivo.

—Veo que Chan Li está también tramitando la tarjeta verde. ¿Cómo es posible? Una estudiante extranjera sin trabajo no tiene opción alguna al permiso de residencia en este país.

—Le dije que Chan Li es un caso especial...

—Sí, lo recuerdo muy bien, pero no me dijo el motivo.

Mr. Smith meditó unos segundos y empezó a articular sus frases con una calculada parsimonia.

—Chan Li es una disidente política, y la Universidad se ha comprometido a ayudarla, pero de forma confidencial. Usted ya me entiende.

—Pues no, la verdad es que no entiendo. Podría ser más explícito.

—Me va a tener que disculpar pero no puedo revelarle esa información... —se irguió de pronto, puso en orden los papeles en la carpeta amarilla y los restituyó al archivador que cerró con llave—. Y ahora, si me lo permite, debo regresar a casa de inmediato. Mi familia me está esperando para cenar.

—No faltaba más.

Convencida de que poco más podía sonsacar al señor reticente, decidí levantarme deprisa de mi silla y adelantarme para abrir la puerta. Mientras cedía ceremoniosa el paso a Mr. Smith, giré discreta el resorte de seguridad de la puerta para dejarla abierta. Había decidido regresar aquella misma noche a la oficina para indagar por mi cuenta en el fichero Chan Li. Mr. Smith pareció contrariado con mi iniciativa de cederle el paso, pero se dejo hacer. Me divirtió su gesto. Nos despedimos a la entrada del edificio con un saludo neutro.

Empieza a anochecer. De camino al apartamento me da la impresión de que alguien me sigue. Cuando encuentro la oportunidad propicia me giro y nada, no puedo ver a nadie. Quizás mi imaginación. En los límites del campus, desprotegidos de gente y patrullas, siento a mi espalda el sonido próximo de unos pasos. Calculo sus cadencias y compruebo que coinciden con las mías. Definitivamente me siguen. Pero detrás de mí no parece haber nadie. Sin poder evitarlo me pongo un poco nerviosa. No pierdo de vista la señal azul del teléfono de alarma, quizás el último de la zona que la Universidad instala en los alrededores del campus para protección de sus retoños. Los pasos repican implacables en la calle desierta y yo cada vez camino más deprisa. Llego a la altura del teléfono pero decido no detenerme. Unos metros más y en casa. Vamos, Alma, sólo unos metros más. Me siento palpitar con fuerza ante la sensación de peligro. Me apresuro. Un vecino está a punto de entrar en mi portal. «¡Espere!», grito y le alcanzo a la carrera, visiblemente aliviada. Antes de entrar, el bulto de siempre me pide monedas. En la oscuridad, una figura borrosa se desvanece.

«China 1989».

Antes de presionar la tecla Enter del ordenador me invade el sentimiento de anticipación y certeza. De inmediato aparecen los rótulos alusivos: China 1989, la plaza Tiananmen abarrotada de jóvenes esperanzados. Se sientan y entonan canciones de libertad, de paz, catapultados por la energía colectiva. En la sentada multitudinaria culminan meses de esperanza y lucha. De los puntos más diversos del país han llegado estudiantes febriles convencidos de la necesidad de un cambio, del poder de su pacífica protesta.

De repente aparecen los tanques. Siguen accediendo por las calles, y avanzan, aplastan, quiebran. Los militares empiezan a difundir el terror. Los muchachos y muchachas gritan, incapaces de modular la magnitud de la brutal pesadilla. La sangre permanece aferrada a las calles durante muchos días. La masacre de Tiananmen es historia y tragedia, repetida en las imágenes inexorables de Internet.

Todavía aturdida, apago el ordenador y regreso a la oscuridad de mi cuarto. Ya es de noche. Las calles empiezan a despertar del letargo. Me pongo zapatillas de deporte y tejanos, aseguro el revólver a mi cintura, las esposas en mi bolsillo trasero, por si se tercia la ocasión, y me deslizo entre los grupos de jóvenes con jaqueca dispuestos a repetirse a sí mismos la noche del sábado. Me dirijo con paso rápido a la oficina de estudios internacionales. Nadie parece seguirme ahora. Entro decidida en el edificio y, después de asegurarme de que no hay nadie, abro la oficina sin dificultad. Manipulo también el cerrojo del archivador y accedo a él sin problemas.

Lepeltier, Lewinter... Li. En la carpeta de Chan Li están los documentos que me había enseñado Smith, pero también aquéllos a los que había aludido; documentos políticos que la acusan de colaboración antirrevolucionaria. Li asociada con uno de los líderes de la plaza de Tiananmen, asesinado en el encuentro. Revisando los papeles se cae una fotografía al suelo. Le doy la vuelta y reconozco en el gesto de Chan Li la misma reproducción que tenía Miguel en su cuarto, la plaza Tiananmen al fondo, pero ahora junto al profesor Martínez. Era obvio que Miguel había escaneado la fotografía y decidido sustituir al profesor por él mismo. Pensé que los documentos de Martínez, también extranjero, debían de estar por allí. Decidí entonces buscar en el archivador la carpeta de Martínez.

Augusto Javier Martínez tenía un historial envidiable. Sus documentos, estrictamente referidos a asuntos de inmigración, aludían sin embargo a numerosos galardones académicos y también humanitarios. Durante el curso 87-88 había asistido como profesor visitante a la Universidad de Hunan, en Changsha, China. Entre los formularios y papeles de su visita encontré un documento relativo a Chan Li que juzgué traspapelado, quizás a propósito. El citado documento contradecía la evidencia de la foto que había encontrado en la carpeta de Li, y en cierto modo justificaba las reservas del remilgado Smith...

Además de los documentos concernientes a su viaje a China, en la carpeta de Martínez se encontraban también aquéllos del proceso de solicitud de la llamada «tarjeta verde», proceso que permite la legalización laboral del inmigrante, admitiéndolo como residente permanente en los Estados Unidos. En el formulario I-485 de la solicitud advertí una interesante disonancia a la serie de negativas rutinarias, aquéllas referidas a preguntas tales como «¿Ha ejercido en los últimos diez años la prostitución, inducido a la prostitución, o planea hacerlo en el futuro?», o bien: «¿Ha estado involucrado en espionaje o tiene intención de involucrarse en actos de espionaje y/o terrorismo?». La disonancia a esas negativas derivaba de la pregunta siguiente: «¿Ha sido alguna vez arrestado, citado por el juez, acusado, o encarcelado por haber quebrantado la ley?». La respuesta marcaba el casillero afirmativo: «Yes».

Cuando estoy a punto de averiguar el motivo de la inculpación y posible arresto de Martínez, se abre la puerta con estrépito y se abalanzan contra mí dos moles uniformadas que me arrastran hacia la salida. Junto a la sorpresa inicial, advierto también la coincidencia irónica con el episodio del malogrado profesor que apunto estaba de desentrañar. Esposada, me meten de cabeza en el coche patrulla y el más grande me da una palmada en el culo. Le llamo cabrón.

El recinto donde me llevaron supuse que era una especie de antesala de la prisión. Mi celda era pequeña, con apenas un retrete, lavabo y catre que parecían formar parte de una misma pieza de metal. La superficie brillaba y olía a desinfectante. Frente a los barrotes de mi celda, a muy poca distancia, estaba la pared amarillenta de aquel recinto que imaginé provisional. Si me apretaba contra los barrotes podía ver, a la izquierda, un trozo de escritorio y una silla desocupada. La oficial de turno parecía aburrida, y de vez en cuando se paseaba por el cuarto silbando una canción de moda. El uniforme que llevaba debía de tener como dos tallas menos de las que precisaba la enorme susodicha, y prometía estallar de un momento a otro bajo la presión de sus rotundas formas.

—Disculpe, pero aquí hay un malentendido —aventuré por enésima vez sin esperanza alguna—. Verá, yo soy investigadora privada y le exijo que me den una explicación. Tengo mis derechos, joder —el exabrupto me salió inapropiado y fatal.

La mujer no me hacía el menor caso.

Por fin se abrió una puerta. Dos señores con actitud algo más amable, o en cualquier caso menos indiferente, me sacaron de la celda y me dirigieron por un interminable pasillo a una pequeña habitación. Que me tranquilizara que todo aquello era mero trámite. En la habitación, equipada para el efecto, me hicieron las fotos de rigor, ésas del letrerito negro de las familiares pelis. Redundante es decir que valoré en muy poco la asociación del momento a los intrépidos filmes. De frente, perfil izquierdo, perfil derecho. Seguro que saldría de desahucio, dada la pinta que llevaba y mi malísimo humor. Aquello pasaba de castaño oscuro. Jorobada y molesta con el ritual, exijo ver a un superior. «¡Tranquilícese señorita!», «¡Cómo que me tranquilice! ¡Esto es un atropello! ¡Y el señorito será usted!», etcétera, etcétera. De vuelta en mi celda, permiten que me siente en el escritorio. Se largan los sabuesos y me quedo a solas con la robusta poli. Nos seguimos ignorando.

—¿Tiene un boli? —aventuré a pedirle sin convicción.

Para mi sorpresa, me extendió un rotulador azul que llevaba en el bolsillo de su apretada camisa.

No le di las gracias.

Había pasado una media ahora de soledad y tamborileo sobre la maltratada mesa del escritorio, cuando volvió a abrirse la puerta y un señor bajito y gordete se me presentó:

—Buenas noches. Soy el comisario Peña, de narcóticos, y éste es mi asistente Wild. ¿Qué tal?

—Pues qué quiere que le diga...

Abstraída como estaba en los sabrosos graffiti del escritorio, la mayoría en español, me daba ya un poco igual lo que fuera a añadir aquel renovado dúo. Había estado haciendo dibujitos y conjeturando sobre las frases malsonantes y enigmáticas de mis predecesores. Por alguna coincidencia inescrutable, se parecían en estilo y tono a las que suelen adornar las puertas de las letrinas: «Pedro, eres un cabrón, pero te adoro»; «Virjensita mia, dame coraje en este mal paso»; «La vida es larga y dura, pues cómeme la vida»; «Por mi madre que te rajo te rajo te rajo»... No faltaba tampoco la popular iconografía de penes en erección junto a corazones atravesados y esbozos de virgencitas. Pero probablemente la mitad de lo que aquí apunto me lo acabé por inventar, dado mi lastimado estado de conciencia en la citada ocasión.

—Disculpe el trato pero era obligado. Tuvimos que comprobar sus credenciales. ¿Así que está investigando el caso Martínez? —el tal Peña me increpaba zalamero. Volví en mí.

—Pues sí, y no tengo mucho en claro —aquello podía ponerse interesante—. Quizás ustedes podrían proporcionarme alguna información.

—Eso depende.

—¿De qué?

—Digamos que depende... —miró al asistente, que permanecía inmutable. El aludido tenía aspecto desgarbado. Era alto, muy delgado y tenía una mata enmarañada de cabello rojizo. Pensé divertida que sólo le faltaba el bombín, o le sobraba una oreja...

—A ver —embestí decidida—. Martínez ha sido arrestado hace ya algunos años. ¿Por qué?

—Por rojo.

—¿Y eso qué tiene que ver con narcóticos?

—Ya se sabe con los comunistas, mala gente. Además, encontramos hace poco heroína en el apartamento de Martínez y suficientes conexiones con el exterior.

—¿Para uso personal?

—Demasiada cantidad. Por otra parte, Martínez no se pinchaba.

—Para alguna amiga, quizás —medité en voz alta, pensando inevitablemente en Chan Li.

—Quién, por ejemplo —a Peña se le encendieron lucecitas de pronto y humedeció imperceptible el bigotito ralo.

—... Pues no sé, algún amigo tendría adicto a la heroína.

—Me parece que usted sabe más de lo que dice. Le convendría informarnos de sus averiguaciones. Sería más prudente —el poli pareció decepcionarse con mi respuesta y recuperó el aburrido tono oficial.

—Y si no lo hago, ¿qué pasa?

—Pues nada, que se ande con cuidado. Aquí gustan poco las forasteras preguntonas.

—Mire, no me venga con amenazas. Yo le digo lo que sé: en el bar Miroir hay un trapicheo oculto de porno y drogas.

—Hace tiempo que lo sabemos. Y qué más.

—Pues nada más.

—Suelta el pico muñeca, me joroban las niñatas que van de lista —se arrancó de pronto el flaco en una voz meliflua, completamente incoherente con la amenaza. Me dio por reír. Aquello se parecía cada vez más a una parodia.

—Y a mí los gilipollas que van de machitos —solté a lo bestia, con más curiosidad por comprobar su reacción que por enfado. Al flaco se le incendió el rostro y fue a por mí. Le detuvo el Peña.

Aquello se estaba poniendo al rojo vivo. Afortunadamente llamaron a la puerta y el melifluo permitió con desgana el paso a una bella mujer de cabello lacio, cazadora y minifalda. La jefe del departamento de Lenguas Romances me había venido a buscar. Los sabuesos hicieron gesto de autorizarme a ir. Antes de largarme, asesté:

—Y dejen de ponerme a nadie pisándome los talones. A mí lo que me joroba son los espías. En cuanto a mi arresto, tendrán noticias de mi abogado muy pronto.

Se miraron con cierta perplejidad, se hicieron a un lado con idéntico gesto y nos permitieron pasar.

Antes de salir, recogí en la «recepción» de la comisaría mi revólver y pertenencias, firmé el recibo consecuente y me marché. A mi lado, la profesora seguía sin decir una palabra.

Ya en el flamante coche deportivo, la jefe me miraba con un atisbo de lástima que me resultó irritante. Yo a mi vez observé con curiosidad sus pupilas dilatadas. Parecía cansada y remota. «Los exámenes», dijo. Sacó un pañuelo de papel de su bolso de mano y lo estrujó contra la nariz. «Tampoco me encuentro muy bien», argumentó, muy poco convincente...

—¿Me pasas algo? —solté así de pronto.

—¿Algo de qué?

—Pues algo. De lo que sea. Llevo un día de mierda y todavía me queda toda la noche por delante.

—Pues la verdad es que no sé de qué me hablas —se empezó a poner nerviosa.

—Venga, anda, no me andes con remilgos.

Cogí su bolso, descargué el contenido sobre mis pantalones y fui enumerando el cargamento privado de la profa. ¡Y se había arriesgado con semejante material en la comisaría! Debía de estar super colocada.

—¿Quién te pasa la droga?

—Mira, en eso mejor no te metas.

—¿Hay alguien más de la universidad en esto?

—Este lugar es muy aburrido. Ya son diez años los que llevo aquí. Seguro que igual que yo más de uno se mete algo.

—Ya.

Escogí un aromático pedazo de hachís y empecé a desmenuzarlo en la palma de la mano. Al poco tenía en mis labios un maravilloso canuto que inhalaba y humedecía con vehemencia. Delicioso. Se lo pasé a la profe de poesía que hizo lo propio. Aparcadas en propiedad oficial, fumábamos en el más perfecto de los silencios.

Todavía quedaban un par de horas para la cita nocturna y decidí tomar una ducha fría y finalizar la serie de vídeos que el difunto había estado viendo los días previos a su muerte. Las películas reiteraban la misma sensualidad, la misma ideología pseudocomunista, los mismos juegos de luces y de colores horteras de los ambiguos personajes de Almodóvar. Nada en claro, quizás tan sólo una obsesión privada del viejo Martínez, hasta cierto punto también ambigua. En una de las secuencias urbanas del cineasta manchego advierto un detalle que me resultaba familiar. Rebobino y congelo la secuencia. Aplicando un papel a la pantalla, reproduzco el contorno de un tosco dibujo.

Hacía una noche atiborrada de estrellas. Apreté mi pistola contra mi cuerpo, haciéndome recordar su presencia a pesar de todo muy poco tranquilizadora. El punto de encuentro era el callejón trasero del bar Miroir.

Esperé unos minutos fumándome un pitillo en aquella noche fresca que auguraba el verano. Recordé momentos similares en geografías diversas, momentos de meditación y cansancio. Aspiro y exhalo el humo con deleite enrarecido de ansiedad. Quizás todo se decida esta noche, quizás mañana mismo pueda marcharme de aquel lugar diminuto donde las buenas intenciones y las alianzas con tabúes morales o políticos se pagaban con la vida. O a lo mejor Martínez había realmente utilizado a Chan Li para su propio interés, pero me parecía poco probable... La guardiana del Miroir, quizás...

Un sonido metálico reverbera a mi espalda. Me vuelvo y me encuentro enfrentada a una figura alta oscurecida contra la luz intensa de un farol de la calle. La proporción coincide, calculo, con la persona que la noche anterior había penetrado a Chan Li. Una voz distorsionada en modulaciones guturales me exige en inglés que abandone el caso, que olvide a Chan Li, que ella es sólo suya y ni la Universidad ni el profesor podían robársela.

—¿Por eso mataste al profesor? Porque quería liberarse de ti y liberar también a Chan Li —aventuré, sin saber muy bien lo que estaba proponiendo.

Noto el recelo en su proximidad amenazante. Mecánicamente aprieto el arma en mi bolsillo. Un destello en la noche señala el filo de un enorme cuchillo. Calculo rápidamente posibilidades y salto a un lado, evitando a propósito hacer uso de mi pistola. Pero antes de poder poner en práctica mis argucias, un golpe brutal reduce aquel cuerpo a una masa oscura a mis pies. Cae un objeto que suena en la calle con el sonido rotatorio de un bate de béisbol. El sonido reverbera en la noche reiterado y preciso, suspendido de todo murmullo. Mientras la realidad despierta de su breve letargo, advierto, frente a mí, la presencia de Chan Li visiblemente relajada, como si despertara de una larga pesadilla de dependencia y angustias. Chan Li me mira con gesto de complicidad. Retuve su mirada un instante y fue entonces cuando empecé a comprender todo con una nitidez sin fisuras.

Un muchacho solitario rondando por la zona advierte la extraña escena, suelta un par de tacos y cuando veo que reacciona le ordeno dar aviso a una ambulancia y a la policía. Registro entonces rápidamente los bolsillos del cuerpo derrumbado de Michael Keith. Encuentro una docena de papelinas y también un folio arrugado, con un poema escrito con la misma grafía que había visto reproducida en notas y documentos. Mientras le ajusto las esposas a Miguel, noto las luces de la patrulla aproximándose. Ni ganas de verles. Dejo a Chan Li junto al cuerpo inconsciente de su amante asesino y regreso a mi cuarto confiando en que el futuro de Li se suture del todo.

De camino a casa, despliego el poema de Martínez:

> *Deslizándome por el vértice*
> *perfecto de tu espalda*
> *Por el ángulo ondulante*
> *de mi decrepitud*
> *apenas puedo modularte sin herirme*
> *Mi querido amor atravesado*
> *de alambre y de metal*
> *metal que te penetra mientras quedo*
> *exhausto de mi contemplación*
> *de mi total ausencia*
> *de ti.*

El viejo Martínez enamorado, el profesor entregado a
filantropías y metáforas finiseculares de perversión y
locura. Combinación quizás perfecta en un lugar apar-
tado y oscuro de Estados Unidos. El precio de la con-
tradicción quizás fue su muerte y una firma obscena
en su nalga izquierda, un diseño arrebatado y salvaje como los textos de urinarios o pupitres, laberintos
gráficos de ansiedad y pasión.

Ya en mi cuarto, llamo a la policía y preparo un in-
forme detallado mientras en la televisión se suceden
las imágenes distorsionadas de un canal pornográfico
privado al que el dueño del apartamento, al parecer, no
estaba abonado. En la distorsión, los cuerpos amon-
tonados de hombres y mujeres, figuras hermafroditas,
gemían en ondulaciones surrealistas.

Llamo a Pedro. Antes de decir nada me advierte el
desinterés total de la empresa contratante. Le pregun-
to si quiere saber el resultado de mi investigación y no
parece muy entusiasmado.

—¿Alguien del departamento? —me pregunta—.
¿La Chair quizás? Siempre me pareció un poco quin-
qui... ¿O alguien tal vez del Miroir?

—Pues siempre tan agudo, Pedro. No, ni la Chair,
ni mucho menos nadie del Miroir; después de todo, se
necesita carnet y autorización para entrar en el laboratorio de idiomas. En el fondo se trata de un crimen
pasional bastante común. Durante su estancia en China, Martínez había conocido a Chan Li y había iniciado
el largo y complejo proceso que permitiría a la aveza-

da estudiante de español asistir a los cursos de doctorado del Midwest College. El suceso de Tiananmen, en cuya sentada había participado el propio Martínez, había precipitado los acontecimientos. El compañero de Li había sido asesinado en el encuentro, y Chan Li hubiera seguido pasos similares si no hubiera sido por la diligencia del profesor Martínez y la discreta colaboración de la Universidad para sacarla de China de inmediato. Para ello habían redactado un documento que afirmaba que Chan Li no había participado en la sentada, y así facilitar la salida del país. Por otra parte, ese tipo de manejos seguramente fueron frecuentes en el periodo que siguió a la masacre, pero el encargado de la oficina de estudios internacionales prefería que no indagara en semejantes trámites.

—¿Y entonces?

—Miguel sentía devoción por Martínez desde hacía mucho tiempo, tardé en darme cuenta, y ése es uno de los motivos por los que decidió seguir de estudiante tanto tiempo, para estar cerca de Martínez. Pero Martínez se mantuvo siempre estricto y distante, quizás por prurito profesional. Cuando llegó Chan Li y Miguel intuyó que le quitaba terreno, se vengó precisamente amándola con absoluta devoción, e indirectamente metiéndola en las drogas.

—¿Cómo fue eso?

—Miguel era quien llevaba el negocio de la heroína en el pueblo, y se lo había montado con los del Miroir, espectáculo porno y todo. Seguro que le metió a Martínez la heroína en su casa para complicarle la vida. Cuando a Martínez lo inculparon y supo de las movidas de Miguel, probablemente se enfureció con él y lo emplazó a una cita en el Miroir la noche del asesinato. Martínez amenazó con denunciar a Miguel y éste decidió matarlo. Por lo demás, Miguel llevaba bastante tiempo preocupado con Martínez. Miguel sabía que el apoyo de Martínez a Chan Li era definitivo para la carrera de la muchacha. La tesis estaba a punto de acabar y muy probablemente conseguiría trabajo en algún lugar de Estados Unidos. Lo del dibujo lo sacó Miguel de una pintada que aparece en una de las películas del repertorio de Martínez, de la cual el chico tiene copia en su casa.

—¿Y qué pasa con Chan Li?

—La chica se ha estado dejando hacer, impelida quizás por un sentimiento de alienación y amargura. Creo que todavía no ha superado la muerte de sus compañeros y el sentimiento de fracaso y pérdida ante la masacre de Pekín. Probablemente se siente aturdida y desesperanzada, en particular tras el asesinato de Martínez. Muerto Martínez, moría no sólo su apoyo moral sino también la alternativa por lo menos inmediata de conseguir salir de la universidad, eventualidad conveniente para el desesperado Miguel quien había ido notando el desprendimiento progresivo de Chan Li. Miguel probablemente sabe también que Chan Li está procurando por su cuenta la tarjeta verde, paradójicamente con el apoyo gubernamental de China que ha facilitado ese tipo de transacciones tras la masacre.

—¡Pero cuánto morbo! Así que todos tenían una doble vida en ese lugar perdido.

—Qué quieres que te diga. Definitivamente, lo que llamas «doble vida» no es una prerrogativa urbana. Tanto el profe como la chica y el novio de la chica tenían de algún modo una doble vida. El primero trató de ayudar a la segunda, o viceversa. De todos modos, en el pozo de heroína en que Chan Li se ha metido participan otros grados de dependencia. El profesor quiso ayudarla al tiempo que se ayudaba a sí mismo. Y Mike no pudo soportar que la muchacha se le escapara de su propia obsesión...

Cuelgo el teléfono y recupero de mi bolsillo el poema del profesor atormentado y observo el reverso del mismo. Las metáforas de su trabajo, del apocalipsis de fin de siglo, permanecían en el dibujo distorsionado de un pene en erección dolorosamente penetrado por una jeringa.

FIN

About the Author /
Acerca de la autora

Alm@ Pérez (pseudonym of Tina Escaja) is an award-winning destructivist/a cyber-poet@, digital artist and scholar based in Burlington, Vermont. Her creative work transcends the traditional book form, leaping into digital art, robotics, augmented reality and multimedia projects exhibited in museums and galleries internationally. Translated into six languages, her poetry, fiction and hypertext have appeared in numerous collections. Some of her works are available on **www.tinaescaja.com**.

Alm@ Pérez (pseudónimo de Tina Escaja) es una galardonada ciber-poet@ destructivist/a, artista digital y profesor universitaria que reside en Burlington, Vermont. Su trabajo creativo transciende el formato en papel y ha sido expuesto en sus variantes multimedia, robótica y de realidad aumentada en museos y galerías internacionales. Selecciones de su trabajo poético, digital y narrativo han aparecido en múltiples colecciones, y ha sido traducido a seis idiomas. Parte de sus creaciones puede accederse en su página personal, **www.tinaescaja.com**.

www.ingramcontent.com/pod-product-compliance
Lightning Source LLC
Chambersburg PA
CBHW021025120726
47905CB00009B/3189